Miracles of Love

Miracles of Love

French Fairy Tales by Women

EDITED BY
Nora Martin Peterson

TRANSLATED BY
Jordan Stump

The Modern Language Association of America
New York   2022

MLA and the MODERN LANGUAGE ASSOCIATION are trademarks
owned by the Modern Language Association of America. For information
about obtaining permission to reprint material from MLA book
publications, send your request by mail (see address below) or e-mail
(permissions@mla.org).

Library of Congress Cataloging-in-Publication Data

Names: Peterson, Nora Martin, editor. | Stump, Jordan, 1959– translator.
Title: Miracles of love : French fairy tales by women / edited by Nora
Martin Peterson ; translated by Jordan Stump.
Other titles: Prodiges d'amour. English.
Description: New York : The Modern Language Association of
America, 2022. | Series: Texts and translations, 1079-2538 ; 38 |
Includes bibliographical references. | Summary: "An English translation
of fairy tales published by women in seventeenth-century France.
Explores themes of love, marriage, sexuality, gender relations, and
female education and literacy. Includes works by Catherine Bernard,
Catherine Durand, Charlotte-Rose Caumont de La Force, Marie-Jeanne
L'héritier de Villandon, and Henriette-Julie de Castelnau, comtesse de
Murat, with brief biographies of the authors"—Provided by publisher.
Identifiers: LCCN 2021014598 (print) | LCCN 2021014599 (ebook) |
ISBN 9781603295741 (paperback) | ISBN 9781603295758 (EPUB)
Subjects: LCSH: Fairy tales—France—Translations into English. |
French fiction—Women authors—Translations into English. |
French fiction—17th century—Translations into English. |
LCGFT: Fairy tales.
Classification: LCC GR161 .P7613 2022 (print) | LCC GR161 (ebook) |
DDC 398.20944—dc23
LC record available at https://lccn.loc.gov/2021014598
LC ebook record available at https://lccn.loc.gov/2021014599

Texts and Translations 38
ISSN 1079-2538

Cover illustration: Detail of Jean-Marc Nattier (French, 1685–1766),
Princesse de Rohan, 1741, oil on canvas, 57 1/8 × 44 1/2 in. (145 × 113 cm),
Toledo Museum of Art (Toledo, Ohio). Purchased with funds from the
Libbey Endowment, Gift of Edward Drummond Libbey, 1952.64.

Published by The Modern Language Association of America
85 Broad Street, Suite 500, New York, New York 10004-2434
www.mla.org

Contents

Introduction vii

Collections in First Fairy Tale Vogue (1690–1703) xxi

Source Texts and Other Editions Consulted xxiii

Suggested Reading xxv

Translator's Note xxix

Catherine Bernard 3
Tufty Riquet 7

Catherine Durand 19
A Miracle of Love 21

Charlotte-Rose Caumont de La Force 59
Green and Blue 63

Marie-Jeanne L'héritier de Villandon 87
The Quick-Witted Princess; or, Finette's Adventures 91
The Wonders of Eloquence; or, The Virtues of a Civil Tongue 126

Henriette-Julie de Castelnau, Comtesse de Murat 161
The Pleasant Punishment 165
Anguillette 194

Works Cited in Headnotes and Footnotes 243

Introduction

From "once upon a time" to "happily ever after," fairy tales remain well-loved in the popular imagination. Many of the fairy tales that readers would first associate with the genre come from Charles Perrault, who is celebrated for having written the definitive French versions of such classics as "Cinderella," "Little Red Riding-Hood," and "Puss in Boots." But during Perrault's own time, the genre of the fairy tale and its influence in France were, in fact, distinctly female.

The end of the seventeenth century saw an explosion of literary fairy tales. Nearly two-thirds of these tales published in France between 1690 and 1709 were authored by women (a group referred to as the *conteuses*). It is important to note that two competing models for the genre—that of Perrault, on the one hand, and that of the *conteuses*, on the other—came into existence at nearly the same time. But from the late seventeenth century until the Revolution, it was the latter model and the latter set of authors that exemplified the genre (Seifert and Stanton 5). Marie-Catherine d'Aulnoy, a contemporary and acquaintance of Perrault, wrote tales that were tremendously popular, with print runs and reprints that equaled or surpassed Perrault's both in France and in England (Palmer and Palmer 232). The themes, style, and audience of these *contes* have a rich and complex history that goes far beyond the associations that many readers have with the fairy tale genre, and in the last few decades, they have increasingly been the subject of critical attention. This volume seeks to acknowledge the literary and cultural significance of the *conteuses* and to restore them to their rightful place in the tradition of French fairy tales. Making these tales more accessible both in their original French and in translation will give readers and students the ability to interact with a larger piece of the context surrounding the literary fairy tale genre of the seventeenth century.

The *contes* of the 1690s were uniquely influenced by and reflective of oral and literary traditions. Oral storytelling was seen as a female activity, often linked by image and metaphor to the female craft of spinning (Seifert and Stanton 2), yet the *contes'* textual origins and influences are equally clear. The availability of printed texts to an increasingly literate public and (relatedly) the increasing number of texts printed in the vernacular for entertainment made fairy tales easy to publish and disseminate. Collections of short novellas, embedded in a framing device, were hugely popular beginning in the Italian Renaissance. The *conteuses* were heavily influenced by the Italian stories of Giovan Francesco Straparola and Giambattista Basile (Trinquet 100–08). Indeed, nearly seventy-five percent of the *contes* that can be traced to popular sources have Italian origins. Straparola's *Le piacevoli notti* (*Pleasant Nights*) was written between 1550 and 1553 and translated into French shortly thereafter. In it, a group of men and women gather on the Venetian island of Murano during carnival to tell jokes, sing songs, resolve riddles, and weave tales. The novellas of the female storytellers in particular emphasize the marvelous and revolve around a maxim or a moral, as do many of the French *contes*, though not always explicitly so. Henriette-Julie de Castelnau, comtesse de Murat, claims in the "Avertissement" of her *Histoires sublimes et allégoriques* (*Sublime and Allegorical Stories*) that "everybody, including herself, was taking their stories from [Straparola]" (Bottigheimer, "France's First Fairy Tales" 23).

Though the *conteuses* do not mention Basile by name, the similarities between their stories and Basile's *Lo cunto de li cunti* (1634–36; *The Tale of Tales*) are evident, and recent work has been done to trace the travels, circulation, and reception of Basile's *contes* in France (Trinquet 100–08). In *Lo cunto de li cunti*, a collection of fifty stories told over five days, the frame narrative is itself a fairy tale, revolving around the adventures and misadventures of a princess named Zoza. Basile's stories, like their French counterparts, reveal a fascination with neologisms, maxims, and the marvelous. Nancy Canepa calls them "bawdy and irreverent but also tender and whimsical; acute in psychological characterization and at the same time encyclopedic in description" (3). Like the tales produced by the *conteuses*, Basile's tales were not written for children, intended instead to be shared at elite courtly gatherings (15).

The dissemination of tales, including the influential collection of Straparola beginning in the sixteenth century, was a process dependent on print technology, and the origins and popularity of the early modern fairy tales are as linked to the history of the book in Europe as they are to the oral transmission processes so frequently associated with the genre. As Ruth Bottigheimer writes, "Fairy tales, as we have come to know them in the modern world, resulted from multiple intersections of technological, commercial, and social processes—printing, publishing, book distribution, and story dissemination" ("Ultimate Fairy Tale" 59). Elsewhere, Bottigheimer suggests somewhat controversially that there is "no evidence to suggest that simple people were telling each other fairy tales" ("France's First Fairy Tales" 18); rather, fairy tales of the "restoration and rise type" were introduced in the late sixteenth and early seventeenth centuries through the book trade (19). While Bottigheimer's hypothesis has been contested, it cannot be denied that at the time of their publication, these *contes*, now largely forgotten, were hugely popular—especially in France, but also in translations that were printed in England and Germany. In particular, d'Aulnoy's tales met with resounding success abroad; her collections were repeatedly reprinted in England, and, like Perrault, d'Aulnoy entered the popular print culture of the *bibliothèque bleue* (Bottigheimer, "Ultimate Fairy Tale" 65).[1] Evidence suggests that women were just as likely as men to be included in literary anthologies and collections of tales until the early nineteenth century (DeJean 57–58). So, what changed? Why did women, who dominated and shaped the genre in their own time, disappear from anthologies, editions, and the collective memory? Over the course of the nineteenth century, fairy tales were increasingly inscribed into the domain of children's literature. Perrault's pithier, moralizing stories came back into favor and became the definitive collection in the French tradition. Other European anthologies, like those of the Grimm brothers beginning in 1812, and Hans Christian Andersen in 1835–37, followed a similar model and rose in popularity as interest in folk collections grew. With the advent of film technology and the rise of the Disney empire, the fairy tale canon slipped further toward the simplified, clean sort of tale and away from the complex plot lines, dramatic violence, and textuality that were written into the literary tales. As Lewis C. Seifert and Domna C. Stanton write in *Enchanted Eloquence*, the desires of readers beginning in the nineteenth century "left little room for the 'complex' tales of the *conteuses*" (37). For nearly two hundred years—double the period of Sleeping Beauty's slumber—the *conteuses* slipped into oblivion, with the occasional exception of d'Aulnoy's tales.[2]

The situation began to change again, at least in the critical reception of the *conteuses*, in the 1970s. When Jacques Barchilon and Raymonde Robert wrote comprehensive typologies and studies of the genre and its development, fairy tales began to attract more serious and scientific attention. In the last decades of the twentieth century, new attention was paid to the *conteuses* for their link to women's writing; critical reevaluation of feminist studies, sexuality, and women writers fit nicely with the monograph-length studies on the *conteuses* published by such scholars as Seifert, Patricia Hannon, Sophie Raynard, and Holly Tucker. These scholars examine the configurations of gender and sexuality, the construction of identity, the *conteuses'* role in redefining women's intellectual and public lives, and the relationship between the tales and medical theories, respectively. Moreover, by the end of the twentieth century, the rising interest in fairy tale scholarship led to an acknowledgment of the genre's complexity; no more would these tales be dismissed as trivial children's literature. Increasingly, fairy tales are being considered for their significant contributions to the political, social, and literary movements of the seventeenth century, a fact that is reflected in the most recent scholarship concerning the tales.

It is important to consider several coexisting trends when tracing the evolution of the literary fairy tale. First, the genre developed alongside that of the novel; as such, it is a primarily literary genre. In d'Aulnoy's "L'île de la félicité" ("The Island of Happiness")—the *conte* embedded within *L'histoire d'Hypolite* (*The Story of Hippolytus*), in which the term *conte de fées* ("fairy tale") appears for the first time—the fairy tale is introduced as written rather than oral, a textual call to arms that d'Aulnoy sounded in order to encourage other *salonnières*—participants in literary salons—to join in the sociopolitical debates of the late seventeenth century (Stedman 33). The *conteuses* who participated in the ensuing explosion of tales took this call to heart: dystopian, hyperbolic, and primarily serious in their tone and message, these fairy tales are closer to literary novellas than to Perrault's often comparatively pithy texts.

Another debate that was at the surface of intellectual conversations at the turn of the eighteenth century was the *querelle des anciens et des modernes* ("quarrel of the ancients and moderns"). The quarrel pitted the merits of ancient Greek and Roman tropes against those of modern visual art, literature, philosophy, and science. After a public confrontation with the chief advocate for the ancients, Nicolas Boileau-Despréaux, Perrault became the champion of the moderns, in particular through his *Parallèle des anciens et des modernes* (1688–94; *Comparison of the Ancients and the Moderns*) (Seifert and Stanton 8–12).[3] The *conteuses'* texts came under regular attack from Boileau, who alternated between explicit scrutiny of specific individuals such as Madeleine de Scudéry and a more "general condemnation of marriage, women, and especially the role of women in the socio-cultural public sphere" (Duggan 130). His satires associate women with some of the common metaphors and images of the day: bestiality, sexuality, and the devil (134). Though the *conteuses* did not explicitly enter the debate, their emphasis on French oral folk sources and on the value of *divertissement* (entertainment) in the tales inscribe them firmly into the modern tradition. Nevertheless, many of the *conteuses* do rely heavily on Greek and Roman mythology and on Ovid's *Metamorphoses*, blending classical characters and tropes together with a distinctly French background.

Equally important to consider are the conditions of production under which these tales were created. Many of the fairy tale writers of the 1690s existed on the margins of Louis XIV's court and were often running from the authorities on account of their scandalous publications or behavior. At the same time, because of their family connections and wealthy patrons, they were uniquely close to court life. Literary salons were places where the *conteuses* could mingle with the intellectual elite of their day, and it was in these salons that the genre originated. Here, writers presented and circulated their tales and could collaborate on new ideas. There is evidence to suggest that Perrault, Basile, and d'Aulnoy presented their tales in their respective academies and literary salons (Bottigheimer, *Fairy Tales* 62). This hypothesis remains controversial, however, and other studies indicate that d'Aulnoy's first collection of *contes* was written during a time of forced solitary confinement in a convent (see Schroeder). Whether or not these tales were created in public spaces, they reflect some of the most pressing social issues and the elevated style of the day.

The *conteuses'* tales employ the *galant* tone, which blended wit, gallantry, and the semblance of an artless natural style.[4] They are also filled with often macabre violence, extraordinary adventures, and bizarre details that go beyond the implausible. They are laced with intertexts connecting them to other artistic productions such as opera, the novel, and the writings of Jean de La Fontaine (Seifert and Stanton 21). The *Histoire d'Hypolite* has many of the same characteristics as other salon-inspired seventeenth-century novels, which suggests that d'Aulnoy "promoted the fairy tale as the latest literary innovation through which a new generation of *mondain* authors could foreground issues important to them as intellectuals and articulate a need for social change" (Stedman 34). The "Riquet" stories by Perrault, Catherine Bernard, and Catherine Durand, as well as "Les enchantements de l'éloquence" ("The Wonders of Eloquence") and Perrault's "Les fées" ("The Fairies"), could certainly have been discussed in this setting, with the respective authors attempting to outperform one another with their literary storytelling games. Self-consciously textual, they experiment with parody, intertextuality, and embodiment. If love remains front and center, and if the formulaic marriage and ensuing happy ending remain common, the path to that ending is often twisted, full of surprises, or laced with a pessimistic view of the capacity to attain true happiness as a woman.

The themes, tone, and context of the 1690s fairy tales strongly resonate with other texts by early modern women writers. The self-awareness these authors show of their status as writers, their critique of various abuses and disadvantages faced by their female characters, and their support of female literacy and education are all important themes in the *querelle des femmes* ("quarrel of the ladies") and in women's writing more generally. Beginning with Christine de Pizan in the fourteenth century, French women writers—and their male counterparts—engaged in a polemical debate about the role of women in society that continued at least until the Revolution (some would argue that it continues to the present day). Lamenting the misogyny of other texts and the mistreatment of women in their everyday lives, the women writers of the *querelle* establish a variety of techniques with which they champion the cause of women and subvert arguments grounded in male misogyny. This is quite evident in tales such as Marie-Jeanne L'héritier de Villandon's "The Wonders of Eloquence," where female education plays a central role, and in Bernard's "Riquet à la houppe" ("Tufty Riquet"), whose author reveals her pessimistic views about love and (forced) marriage. It is also evident in tales such as "L'adroite princesse" ("The Quick-Witted Princess"), in which L'héritier's heroine goes to great and violent lengths in order to protect her virtue. Though there are moments of humor and wit, most of the tales in this volume are serious in tone and intent, emphasizing the corruption, persecution, and unfair treatment that the authors saw in society and, in many cases, in their own lives (Zipes 8–9). These *contes* take their representation of women seriously, and the means they use to discuss the position of women in society are often far from conventional. Even when the tales start and finish in a more or less predictable manner, they take different and often winding, elaborate, and subtly subversive paths to get there (Seifert and Stanton 28).

Our collection begins with Bernard's version of "Tufty Riquet." Today's readers may be acquainted with Perrault's version; indeed, the story, which appears not to have been based on a source text, is almost universally attributed to him. This attribution is strongly misleading. Though scholars have not definitively established the relation between the two texts, it seems evident that Perrault and Bernard wrote their versions simultaneously, perhaps as part of a literary game, or that Perrault based his version on Bernard's (Seifert 205–06). And indeed, there are important differences between the two, differences that shed light on what is missing from our perception of the genre today. In Bernard's much more pessimistic version, readers never doubt Mama's victimization. She does not come to love her husband as the Mama in Perrault's version does. Instead, readers are presented with a commentary on the disappointment and limitations of marriage for women, and perhaps the whisper of a desire to change the status quo (206–11; Hanon 126–31). None of this comes out in Perrault's text, which instead reverts to the gender norms of the day and simplifies—by reversing—the ambivalence of Mama's feelings for Riquet at the end. Thus, by beginning our collection with Bernard's version, we introduce a selection of *contes* that asks different questions (and proposes different solutions) about love, marriage, and gender relations than the ones readers might be accustomed to associating with fairy tales. Our hope is to create a generation of readers that will debate, ask questions, and appreciate the ambiguity with which the genre was imbued in its own day. "Le prodige d'amour"

("A Miracle of Love"), Durand's variation on the "Riquet" story, is even more obscure. To our knowledge, this volume contains the first English translation of this tale to appear. Readers will find a comparative reading of the three "Riquet" tales to be particularly rich.

In order to underscore some of the issues central to these literary fairy tales, we have selected texts that do unexpected things with familiar tropes. Charlotte-Rose Caumont de La Force shows explicit interest in revising the misogynistic representation of female sexuality.[5] In "Vert et Bleu" ("Green and Blue"), both the male and female characters are "participants in the erotic field of vision"; the text underscores the fact that their desire is mutual and can be mutually expressed (Seifert 128–29). The bathing scene, during which the narrative shifts from Vert's gaze on Bleu's nude body to Bleu's realization that Vert is gazing, then back and forth again, would hardly be imaginable from the standpoint of canonical fairy tales. But put in conversation with d'Aulnoy's tales, which frequently focus on the question of female desire, the story shows that women were not writing themselves as objects of desire in fairy tales but as equal participants in "deliberate expressions of . . . physical desire" (129). We hope to show that in their original setting, as texts by women writers, literary fairy tales allowed for and embraced female desire.

The two texts we have included by L'héritier represent some of the most important characteristics of the *conteuses'* tales. "The Quick-Witted Princess" offers a fearless princess unafraid to pursue revenge and to plot bold deeds in defense of her honor. Readers can enjoy trying to reconcile traditional "feminine" virtues such as submission and obedience with a strong princess who undeniably contradicts and subverts "the image of passive and mindless fairy-tale princesses propagated by mass media today" (Seifert and Stanton 27).

"The Wonders of Eloquence" is the tale of a girl who is granted the gifts of a fairy explicitly because of her love of reading, and the ending reinforces the importance of education for women (Hanon 193–99). Of particular interest is L'héritier's conversational framing letter at the beginning of the tale, which situates the text directly into a dialogue between salon women (Stedman 102–03). Within the tale itself, L'héritier distinguishes her tale from Perrault's "Les fées," of which this tale is another variation, by emphasizing literacy as a means to achieving upward mobility, and with her playful suggestion that for women, true power is invested in words and education rather than fairies and magic.

Finally, we have included tales that play with, question, or redefine the genre of the fairy tale as we have commonly come to understand it. Readers who expect a prince and princess, a rescue, or an inevitably happy ending, often thanks to some measure of supernatural intervention, will be surprised by "L'heureuse peine" ("The Pleasant Punishment") and "Anguillette," texts that problematize the efficacy of the formula and that surprise readers with new questions. Both *contes* were written by Murat, a lesbian writer whose scandal-tinged life makes her a perfect candidate for writing dystopian, pessimistic, and subversive fairy tales. By constantly undoing expectations, Murat asks us to reconsider the meaning of love, the efficacy of binaries such as that of good and evil, the existence of serendipity, and the reasons we believe certain things about our lives. Her tales break the rules about gender and give women, in particular, a textual place where they can imagine a different role for themselves or call into question the role they have been given. The increasing availability of the *conteuses'* work is a sign that the tides are changing. By bringing these seven stories together, we hope to give readers a more complete sense of what the fairy tale genre was and to restore these writers' former prominence. We hope to inspire our readers to retell these stories, to read them together with the collections of Perrault and d'Aulnoy, to ask questions, and to revel in the creativity of texts that are simultaneously bizarre, refreshing, elaborate, and provocative.

Notes

1. *Bibliothèque bleue:* a type of popular literature and ephemera printed in France primarily between c. 1602 and c. 1830 that appealed to readers across social strata, including class and sex.

2. Faith E. Beasley's book *Salon, History, and the Creation of Seventeenth-Century France: Mastering Memory* discusses this phenomenon in detail.

3. Perrault's support of women was not without ambivalence, however. See Duggan for an analysis (144–64).

4. The *galant* style emerged late in the seventeenth century and continued throughout the eighteenth century; it was thus fairly new during the time of the first fairy tale vogue. Extending beyond the literary, it was a cultural phenomenon that dominated music, popular culture, and fashion. The literary magazine *Le Mercure galant* exemplified and perpetuated the style.

5. Another example can be found in *Histoire de la Marquise-Marquis de Banneville* (*The Story of the Marquise-Marquis de Banneville*), a delightful gender-bending tale, (likely) written collaboratively by François-Timoléon de Choisy, L'héritier, and Perrault.

Works Cited

Beasley, Faith E. *Salon, History, and the Creation of Seventeenth-Century France: Mastering Memory.* Ashgate, 2006.

Bottigheimer, Ruth. *Fairy Tales: A New History.* State U of New York P, 2009.

———. "France's First Fairy Tales: The Restoration and Rise Narratives of *Les facetieuses nuitz du Seigneur François Straparole.*" *Marvels and Tales,* vol. 19, no. 1, 2005, pp. 17–31.

———. "The Ultimate Fairy Tale: Oral Transmission in a Literate World." *A Companion to the Fairy Tale,* edited by Hilda Ellis Davidson and Anna Chaudhri, D. S. Brewer, 2003, pp. 57–70.

Canepa, Nancy. Introduction. *The Tale of Tales; or, Entertainment for Little Ones*, by Giambattista Basile, translated by Canepa, Wayne State UP, 2007, pp. 1–31.

Choisy, François-Timoléon de, et al. *The Story of the Marquise-Marquis de Banneville*. Edited by Joan DeJean, translated by Stephen Rendall, Modern Language Association of America, 2004.

DeJean, Joan. "Classical Reeducation: Decanonizing the Feminine." *50 Years of Yale French Studies: A Commemorative Anthology Part 2: 1980–1988*, special issue of *Yale French Studies*, no. 97, 1998, pp. 55–70.

Duggan, Anne E. *Salonnières, Furies, and Fairies: The Politics of Gender and Cultural Change in Absolutist France*. U of Delaware P, 2004.

Hannon, Patricia. *Fabulous Identities: Women's Fairy Tales in Seventeenth-Century France*. Rodopi, 1998. Faux Titre 151.

Palmer, Nancy, and Melvin Palmer. "English Editions of French 'Contes de Fées' Attributed to Mme d'Aulnoy." *Studies in Bibliography*, no. 27, 1974, pp. 227–32.

Raynard, Sophie. *La seconde préciosité: Floraison des conteuses, 1690–1756*. Tübingen, Narr, 2002. Biblio 17.

Schroeder, Volker. "Madame d'Aulnoy's Productive Confinement." *Anecdota*, 2 May 2020, anecdota.princeton.edu/archives/1182.

Seifert, Lewis C. *Fairy Tales, Sexuality, and Gender in France, 1690–1715: Nostalgic Utopias*. Cambridge UP, 1996. Cambridge Studies in French 55.

Seifert, Lewis C., and Domna C. Stanton. Introduction. *Enchanted Eloquence: Fairy Tales by Seventeenth-Century French Women Writers*, edited and translated by Seifert and Stanton, Center for Reformation and Renaissance Studies / Iter, 2010, pp. 1–45. The Other Voice in Early Modern Europe: The Toronto Series 9.

Stedman, Allison. "Jean Racine, Marie-Jeanne Lhéritier de Villandon, and Charles Perrault: A Revised Triumverate." *Teaching Seventeenth- and Eighteenth-Century French Women Writers*, edited by Faith E. Beasley, Modern Language Association of America, 2011, pp. 103–08.

Trinquet, Charlotte. *Le conte de fées français, 1690–1700: Traditions italiennes et origines aristocratiques*. Narr Francke Verlag, 2012.

Tucker, Holly. *Pregnant Fictions: Childbirth and the Fairy Tale in Early Modern France*. Wayne State UP, 2003.

Zipes, Jack, translator. *Beauties, Beasts and Enchantment: Classic French Fairy Tales*. Penguin, 1989.

Collections in
First Fairy Tale Vogue (1690–1703)

Marie-Catherine d'Aulnoy, *L'île de la félicité*, 1690

Catherine Bernard, *Inès de Cordoue*, 1695*

Marie-Jeanne L'héritier de Villandon, *Œuvres meslées*, 1695*

Charlotte-Rose Caumont de La Force, *Les contes des contes*, 1697*

Charles Perrault, *Histoires ou contes du temps passé*, 1697

Marie-Catherine d'Aulnoy, *Les contes des fées* (4 vols.), 1697–98

Henriette-Julie de Castelnau, comtesse de Murat, *Contes de fées*, 1698*

Chevalier de Mailly, *Les illustres fées, contes galans*, 1698

Jean de Prechac, *Contes moins contes que les autres*, 1698

Catherine Durand, *La comtesse de Mortane*, 1699

Henriette-Julie de Castelnau, comtesse de Murat, *Histoires sublimes et allégoriques*, 1699

Eustache le Noble, *Le gage touché*, 1700

Catherine Durand, *Les petits soupers de l'esté 1699*, 1702*

Louise de Bossigny, comtesse d'Auneuil, *La tiranie des fées détruite*, 1702

* Works marked with an asterisk are represented in this volume.

Source Texts and Other Editions Consulted

Bernard, Catherine. "Riquet à la houppe." *Inès de Cordoüe: Nouvelle espagnole*, by Bernard, Paris, 1697, pp. 39–62. *Bayerische StaatsBibliothek Digital*, mdz-nbn-resolving.de/urn:nbn:de:bvb:12-bsb10092690-5.

Le cabinet des fées, ou Collection choisie des contes des fées et autres contes merveilleux. Geneva, 1785–89. 41 vols.

Durand, Catherine. "Le prodige d'amour." *Petits soupers de l'esté 1699*, by Durand, Prault Père, 1702, pp. 120–77.

———. "Le prodige d'amour." Robert, pp. 475–95.

La Force, Charlotte-Rose Caumont de. "Vert et Bleu." *Le cabinet des fées*, vol. 6, pp. 103–26. *Gallica*, 2 Aug. 2016, ark:/12148/bpt6k9628496k.

———. "Vert et Bleu." Robert, pp. 372–87.

L'héritier de Villandon, Marie-Jeanne. "Les aventures de Finette." L'héritier de Villandon, *Œuvres meslées*, pp. 229–98.

———. "Les aventures de Finette." Robert, pp. 93–114.

———. "Les enchantements de l'éloquence." L'héritier de Villandon, *Œuvres meslées*, pp. 163–228.

———. "Les enchantements de l'éloquence." Robert, pp. 69–91.

———. *Œuvres meslées.* 1695. *Gallica*, 15 Oct. 2007, ark:/12148/bpt6k62376r.

Murat, Henriette-Julie de Castelnau, comtesse de. "Anguillette." 1698. *Le cabinet des fées*, vol. 1, pp. 271–331. *Gallica*, 3 July 2014, ark:/12148/bpt6k65804141.

———. "Anguillette." Murat, *Contes*, pp. 85–117.

———. *Contes*. Edited by Geneviève Patard, Champion, 2006. Bibliothèque des génies et des fées 3.

———. "L'heureuse peine." 1698. *Le cabinet des fées*, vol. 1, pp. 434–64. *Gallica*, 3 July 2014, ark:/12148/ bpt6k65804141.

———. "L'heureuse peine." Murat, *Contes*, pp. 179–96.

Robert, Raymonde, editor. *Contes*. Champion, 2005. Bibliothèque des génies et des fées 2.

SUGGESTED READING

Sources below are general recommended reading on the *conteuses*, politics and society in absolutist France, and the literary context of the genre's evolution. For suggested reading on each individual author or the tales included in this volume, we have provided a separate reading list following each author's biography in the text.

Instructors may find it useful to teach this volume of tales together with the *contes* of Marie-Catherine d'Aulnoy or Charles Perrault, or both; hence, the volumes by those authors listed below are the ones we have used in our classrooms (both in French and in English translation). The anthology edited by Jack Zipes includes a large number of tales by d'Aulnoy and Perrault, and the anthology edited by Lewis C. Seifert and Domna C. Stanton includes two tales by d'Aulnoy and three of the same texts as our volume. Graduate classes, or classes in literary translation, may benefit from a comparative study of the different translations; please see the list of source texts included in the front matter to this volume.

Bottigheimer, Ruth. *Fairy Tales: A New History*. State U of New York P, 2009.

———. "France's First Fairy Tales: The Restoration and Rise Narratives of *Les facetieuses nuitz du Seigneur François Straparole*." Tucker, *Reframing*, pp. 17–31.

———. "Tale Spinners: Submerged Voices in Grimms' Fairy Tales." *New German Critique: An Interdisciplinary Journal of German Studies*, no. 27, 1982, pp. 141–50.

Brocklebank, Lisa. "Rebellious Voices: The Unofficial Discourse of Cross-Dressing in d'Aulnoy, de Murat, and Perrault." *Children's Literature Association Quarterly*, vol. 25, no. 3, 2000, pp. 127–36.

Canepa, Nancy L., editor. *Teaching Fairy Tales.* Wayne State UP, 2019.

d'Aulnoy, Marie-Catherine. *Contes de fées.* 1697. Edited by Constance Cagnat-Debœuf, Gallimard, 2008.

DeJean, Joan. *Ancients against Moderns: Culture Wars and the Making of a Fin de Siècle.* U of Chicago P, 1997.

———. *Tender Geographies: Women and the Origins of the Novel in France.* Columbia UP, 1991.

Duggan, Anne E. "The Reception of the Grimms in Nineteenth-Century France: *Volkspoesie* and the Reconceptualization of the French Fairy-Tale Tradition." *Fabula*, vol. 55, nos. 3–4, 2014, pp. 260–85.

Feat, Anne-Marie. "Playing the Game of Frivolity: Seventeenth-Century 'Conteuses' and the Transformation of Female Identity." *The Journal of the Midwest Modern Language Association*, vol. 45, no. 2, 2012, pp. 217–42.

Harries, Elizabeth W. *Twice upon a Time: Women Writers and the History of the Fairy Tale.* Princeton UP, 2001.

———. "The Violence of the Lambs." Tucker, *Reframing*, pp. 54–66.

Hoffmann, Kathryn A. "Of Monkey Girls and a Hog-Faced Gentlewoman: Marvel in Fairy Tales, Fairgrounds, and Cabinets of Curiosities." Tucker, *Reframing*, pp. 67–85.

Hofmann, Melissa A. "The Fairy as Hero(ine) and Author: Representations of Female Power in Murat's 'Le Turbot.'" *Marvels and Tales*, vol. 28, no. 2, 2014, pp. 252–77.

Jones, Christine A. "The Poetics of Enchantment." *Marvels and Tales*, vol. 17, no. 1, 2003, pp. 55–74.

———. "Thoughts on 'Heroism' in French Fairy Tales." *Marvels and Tales*, vol. 27, no. 1, 2013, pp. 15–33.

Mainil, Jean. *Madame d'Aulnoy et le rire des fées: Essai sur la subversion féerique et le merveilleux comique sous l'Ancien Régime.* Kimé, 2001.

Perrault, Charles. *The Complete Fairy Tales.* 1697. Translated by Christopher Betts, Oxford UP, 2009.

———. *Contes.* Edited by Jean-Pierre Collinet and Natalie Froloff, Gallimard, 1999.

Reddan, Bronwyn. "Losing Love, Losing Hope: Unhappy Endings in Seventeenth-Century Fairy Tales." *Papers on French Seventeenth-Century Literature*, vol. 42, no. 83, 2015, pp. 327–39.

———. "Scripting Love in Fairy Tales by Seventeenth-Century French Women Writers." *French History and Civilization*, vol. 7, 2016, pp. 97–107.

Robert, Raymonde. *Le conte de fées littéraire en France de la fin du XVIIe siècle à la fin du XVIIIe siècle.* PU de Nancy, 1982.

Schacker, Jennifer. "Unruly Tales: Ideology, Anxiety, and the Regulation of the Genre." *The Journal of American Folklore*, vol. 120, no. 478, 2007, pp. 381–400.

Seifert, Lewis C. "Queer Time in Charles Perrault's 'Sleeping Beauty.'" *Queer(ing) Fairy Tales*, special issue of *Marvels and Tales*, vol. 29, no. 1, 2015, pp. 21–41.

Seifert, Lewis C., and Domna C. Stanton, editors and translators. *Enchanted Eloquence: Fairy Tales by Seventeenth-Century French Women Writers.* Center for Reformation and Renaissance Studies / Iter, 2010. The Other Voice in Early Modern Europe: The Toronto Series 9.

Shippey, Tom. "Rewriting the Core: Transformations of the Fairy Tale in Contemporary Writing." *A Companion to the*

Fairy Tale, edited by Hilda Ellis Davidson and Anna Chaudhri, Brewer, 2003, pp. 253–74.

Stedman, Alison. "D'Aulnoy's *Histoire d'Hypolite, comte de Duglas* (1690): A Fairy-Tale Manifesto." Tucker, *Reframing*, pp. 32–53.

Straparola, Giovan Francesco. *The Pleasant Nights.* 1550–53. Edited and translated by Suzanne Magnanini, Iter, 2015. The Other Voice in Early Modern Europe: The Toronto Series 40.

Trinquet, Charlotte. *Le conte de fées français, 1690–1700: Traditions italiennes et origines aristocratiques.* Narr Francke Verlag, 2012.

Tucker, Holly, editor. *Reframing the Early French Fairy Tale.* Special issue of *Marvels and Tales*, vol. 19, no. 1, 2005.

Zipes, Jack, translator. *Beauties, Beasts and Enchantment: Classic French Fairy Tales.* Penguin, 1989.

———. *The Great Fairy Tale Tradition: From Straparola and Basile to the Brothers Grimm: Texts, Criticism.* W. W. Norton, 2001.

Zuerner, Adrienne. "Disorderly Wives, Loyal Subjects: Marriage and War in Early Modern France." *Dalhousie French Studies*, vol. 56, 2001, pp. 55–65.

Translator's Note

Translators bristle at the idea that their work involves nothing more than a transfer of meaning from one language to another, but even if that's a reductive view of the process it's not exactly false. Its only real weakness is that it takes for granted the meaning of *meaning*. The meaning of a word, for instance, is not limited to the definition we find in the dictionary; it's also to be found in the way that word is used in a given culture or subculture or work, and it's also to be found in that word's place in a larger unit of meaning, from the sentence to the paragraph to the text as a whole. Nor does that "text as a whole" have a meaning that it expresses entirely through its own words: the meaning of the text is also located in its purpose, its audience, the literary tradition it participates in, and on and on. No translation can ever fully "transfer" all that meaning, any more than a single act of reading can account for it all. What translation does is to attempt to *re-create* that meaning, and that attempt involves a great many things, from simply reproducing the sense of the words to evoking the context in which the text uses them to aiming at producing a readerly experience in some sense parallel to the original's, and (again) on and on. There is no one meaning that translation is trying to get across, and no one means for doing so; it's an endless process of negotiation, between one language and another, one voice and another, one experience and another. The text that a translator produces has all the appearances of a stable, definitive work, but in fact it's anything but: it's a provisional, no doubt partial, surely subjective (but still potentially effective) attempt to convey the nature of a massively multifaceted act of language that resists every attempt to reproduce it.

All of this is, I would think, well known to any translator with a little experience, but it came home to me with particular force when I began to translate the fairy tales presented in this volume: they resisted me more than I'm used to. As a reader and a translator I'm strongly inclined toward contemporary writing, particularly of the avant-garde variety; nonetheless, when my colleague Nora Peterson raised the possibility of collaborating on an edition and a translation of these stories I leapt at the chance (however fond I am of the present literary moment, it's nice to step outside it from time to time). On first reading these tales I was happy to find some delightful similarities to the kind of modern writing I love—ironic narrators, playful digressions, teasing ambiguities, a beguiling lack of respect for the fourth wall—but once I sat down to translate them I was surprised by their distance from the kind of writing I spend most of my time with: a different sensibility with respect to the shape of a sentence, a more limited but more openly impassioned vocabulary, a more stylized approach to dialogue . . . I found the stories perfectly readable, entirely accessible, but I struggled to come up with a convincing voice in which to cast them. When I translate contemporary writers, I most often think I have a fairly well-founded idea of what they should sound like in English, but here I felt no such certainty: once I began to translate, these stories seemed to come from such a faraway time, from such a lost tradition, from such distant authors, that I wondered if I could work my way into them.

One of the most important lessons of translation—and one of the reasons I believe works in translation (and the craft of translation) should be more widely taught—is that our difference from other people, other cultures, and other ways of thinking is real but not absolute. The gap can be bridged. Just as these stories show us experiences far removed from our own but not impermeable to our sympathies or irrelevant to our lives, their language—their way of telling stories, their imagination—is not ours, but neither is it irremediably alien to us. We need only take the trouble to find our way into their world, and to let their world into ours.

The only way to do this is to embark on that unending negotiation I referred to earlier. If I've succeeded in translating these stories, it's only because I did what I always do as a translator: first bang out a very literal and very bad first draft, then let time and continual rethinking turn that dross into something that works. Several times I revise that first draft, thinking of the kind of language I would like to read and of the nature of the original text as I recall it; I then compare the results to that original text, this time striving to let the author's language influence the language of the translation. Then I revise it again without the original, and then again with the original, and so forth and so on. In time, with patience, a voice emerges that is neither my voice nor the original's, that partakes of both but that nonetheless has its own identity. It's the translator's very difficult job to make sure that that identity fits with the nature of the narration and of the author, that it respects the voice of the original even as it necessarily departs from it, that it does what the original does, even if it does it differently. It's an arduous process, and fraught with peril, and the end result is, as I say, never definitive, but in my opinion it's always possible, to one degree or another, for the voice of the other to speak in our language in spite of all that separates us.

A perennial dispute in the field of translation involves the degree to which the "foreignness" of a foreign text must be maintained. What has come to be known as a foreignizing translation is one that underscores the original's difference, that makes no attempt to hide the fact that it's a translation, that perhaps seeks to enrich the target language through the introduction of features of the source language; a domesticating translation, on the other hand, seeks to make the text as digestible as possible for a reader of the target language, with every linguistic difference smoothed over, all cultural unfamiliarities erased. Not surprisingly, no one is eager to be thought of as a domesticating translator, but to my mind both of those categories imply a rigidity that should be the opposite of everything translation (and, more broadly, comprehension across cultures) stands for. Just as every one of us speaks in an irreducible blend of the conventional and the idiosyncratic, every translation foreignizes to some degree and domesticates to some degree. I don't believe a translation should strive for either of those poles. I don't believe, for instance, that a translation of a three-hundred-year-old text should try to imitate the literary style of that time, or that it should attempt to update it—any translation produced with one of those two goals in mind will end up causing more cringes than pleasure. Thus, as I translated these stories, I never forgot their age, but I tried to evoke it discreetly; I never sought to impose modern diction, but I found that when brought in at the right time, in small doses, it can evoke an image or a character with particular clarity. Similarly, though as I rule I respected the form of these stories, I did not hesitate to recast a sentence or play with the paragraph breaks when I felt the English-language text was better served by such changes. My allegiance is to the story and to its readers; as a translator I have no rule, ideology, or ambition beyond that.

I only hope that I will have allowed readers to find these stories as surprising, as odd, and as moving as I have. If I have, then there remains only to thank those who made this book possible. Thanks, then, to Nora Peterson, for having proposed this project to begin with, and for her unstinting help, encouragement, and lively discussion; thanks, too, to Eleanor Hardin, for her careful reading of my manuscript, her unerring ear for language, her sensitive suggestions, and everything else.

Miracles of Love

CATHERINE BERNARD

(c. 1663–1712)

Of all the *conteuses* included in this volume, Catherine Bernard wrote the fewest tales—only two—but they were both frequently read and printed well into the eighteenth century. Born into a comfortable Protestant family in Rouen, Bernard moved to Paris before 1680 in order to pursue a literary career. She publicly—and evidently against her family's wishes—converted to Catholicism after the revocation of the Edict of Nantes in 1685, after which point Catholicism was all but obligatory for anyone who aspired be a part of the literary elite in Paris. Bernard was a highly regarded author of four historical novels, a short story, and two plays. Her two fairy tales are embedded in her novel *Inès de Cardoüe* (39–62). This same novel also contains what came to be known as a manifesto for the aesthetic principle of the seventeenth- and eighteenth-century *contes*: the adventures "fussent toujours contre la vraisemblance, et les sentiments toujours naturels" 'should always be implausible and the emotions always natural' (6). She was frequently mentioned in *Le Mercure galant*, and her poetry was anthologized and won competitions sponsored in the 1690s by the Académie Française and by the Académie de Jeux Floraux de Toulouse. She never married, and after publishing *Inès de Cordoüe* she dedicated herself to a pious existence, writing almost exclusively religious poetry.

Bernard's "Riquet à la houppe" ("Tufty Riquet")[1] was written at the same time as Charles Perrault's version; in fact, the chronology of the two *contes* has been a matter of some debate. Many scholars believe that the two versions were written contemporaneously as a friendly competition. Bernard's version is notable for its dyspeptic reading of love as opposed to Perrault's clear-cut, less ambivalent fairy-tale ending. Seen as a way to elevate social rank, marriage was rarely a matter of love and often led to disillusionment among the noble classes, especially in intellectual circles; this pessimism is evident in Bernard's text. In Perrault's version, the unnamed princess learns at the very last minute, from Riquet himself, that she has the power to change the one she loves into the most beautiful man on earth; she and Riquet, both transformed, live happily ever after (282–83). While Perrault's moral at the end of the story makes it unclear whether Riquet has physically transformed or whether it is love itself that changes him in the princess's eyes, the message is both more optimistic and more simplistic than Bernard's in its treatment of the female character.

Further Reading

Bernard, Catherine. *Inès de Cordoüe: Nouvelle espagnole.* 1697. *Bayerische StaatsBibliothek Digital*, mdz-nbn-resolving.de/urn:nbn:de:bvb:12-bsb10092690-5.

Escola, Mark, editor. *Nouvelles galantes du XVIIe siècle.* Flammarion, 2004, pp. 394–408.

Hannon, Patricia. *Fabulous Identities: Women's Fairy Tales in Seventeenth-Century France.* Rodopi, 1998, pp. 126–31. Faux Titre 151.

---

1. Literally (but, in English at least, rather inelegantly) "Riquet with the cowlick."

Piva, Franco. "À la recherche de Catherine Bernard." *Oeuvres de Catherine Bernard*, edited by Franco Piva, vol. 1, Schena, 1993, pp. 15–47.

Ringham, Felizitas. "Riquet à la houppe: Conteur, conteuse." *French Studies: A Quarterly Review*, vol. 52, no. 3, 1998, pp. 291–304.

Seifert, Lewis. "Catherine Bernard (c. 1663–1712)." *The Teller's Tale: Lives of the Classic Fairy-Tale Writers*, edited by Sophie Raynard, State U of New York P, 2013, pp. 208–11.

———. *Fairy Tales, Sexuality, and Gender in France, 1690–1715: Nostalgic Utopias*. Cambridge UP, 1996. Cambridge Studies in French 55.

Vincent, Monique. "Les deux versions de *Riquet à la houppe:* Catherine Bernard (mai 1696), Charles Perrault (octobre 1696)." *Littératures Classiques*, vol. 25, 1995, pp. 299–309.

TUFTY RIQUET

There was once a high nobleman of Granada who owned a treasure befitting his birth, but who had a sorrow in his household that poisoned all the gifts lavished on him by Fortune. His only daughter, born with all the traits that make a woman beautiful, was so simple-minded that beauty itself only made her repellent. Her movements were untouched by any hint of grace. Her person was delicate and yet ungainly, since there was no soul in that body.

Mama, as the girl was named, was not bright enough to see just how dim she was, but she sensed that others scorned her, even if she could not fathom why. One day, out walking alone (as was as her custom), she saw a man emerge from the ground, a man so ugly as to seem a monster. The sight of him made her want to flee, but the words he spoke held her where she was.

"Stop," he said. "I have some unpleasant things to tell you, but some most pleasant things to promise you. You are a very beautiful woman, but along with your beauty there is something about you that turns people away, which is that you have no thought in your head. I don't mean to boast, but that flaw puts you infinitely beneath me, for what is true of your mind is true only of my appearance. That is the cruel thing I had to say to you, but from your dull stare I believe I was expecting too much when I feared I might give offense. I don't expect much, then, from the offer I was intending to make, but I shall venture to make it all the same. Would you like to be smart?"

"Yes," answered Mama, no differently than she would have said "no."

"Well then," he went on, "here is the way. You must love Tufty Riquet—that's my name—and you must marry me in a year's time. That's what I ask of you: think it over, if you can. And if you find you cannot, then you must often repeat the words I am about to tell you; they will teach you, at long last, to think. Goodbye, for a year. Here are the words that will dispel your torpor, and at the same time cure your idiocy:

> You who can bring all things to life,
> Love, if to be no more a dolt
> I need only learn to love,
> Then for that I am ready."

As Mama spoke those words, her body became more animated, her air more alert, her gait more agile. She spoke them again. She went to see her father, and said to him things that were first articulate, then sensible, then bright.[1] So great and so sudden a transformation could not go unnoticed, and all those who noticed now took a new interest in her. Suitors flocked to her in droves; no more was Mama overlooked at the ball; no more was she alone when she went out for a stroll. Jealousies and infidelities came to life all around her; the court spoke only of her, and for her.[2]

Among the many who were drawn to her, it was inevitable that she would find someone more winning than Tufty Riquet; her benefactor was ill repaid for the intelligence he had given her. She faithfully repeated the words he had taught her, and as she did she felt a burgeoning love grow inside her—but despite what their author intended it was not love for him.

Her preference went to the handsomest of her many suitors, who was not the one with the most generous fortune. Her parents had unwittingly wished unhappiness on their daughter when they wished her a sharper mind, and now that it was too late to take that intelligence from her, they tried to at least warn her off love. But forbidding a pretty young girl to love is like forbidding

---

1. Note the crescendo of terms here: Mama's rhetorical skills are improving even as she speaks.

2. Bernard evokes the cultural importance of being well-spoken here; eloquence was a necessary status symbol quite equal to beauty at the French court.

a tree to bear leaves in the month of May:[3] she only loved Arada—for that was her suitor's name—all the more.

She had taken great care to tell no one of the adventure by which reason had come to her. Keeping that secret was of the utmost importance to her vanity; she had by now wit enough to understand the need to maintain the mystery by which she'd acquired it.

But in the meantime, the year that Tufty Riquet had given her to learn to think and make up her mind to marry him had almost run out. Full of dread, she saw the terrible day drawing near. Her intelligence had become a most cruel gift, for now she could not blind herself to the miseries that awaited her: losing her lover forever, finding herself ruled by someone of whom she knew nothing but his ugliness, which was perhaps the least of his defects—someone she had promised to marry by accepting his gifts, gifts that she did not want to return. Such were the reflections forever coursing through Mama's mind.

One day, lost in her thoughts of that cruel fate, she wandered off all alone. She soon heard a great noise, and voices from under the earth singing the words Tufty Riquet had taught her. She shuddered: that was the sign that the fateful day had come. The ground immediately

---

3. In the early modern period, May was the month associated with love and sexuality.

opened up before her, and she hesitantly made her way down the hole until she saw Tufty Riquet, surrounded by others every bit as ugly as he. What a sight for a girl once pursued by all the comeliest men of her land! Her sorrow was even greater than her surprise, and in silence she wept a torrent of tears: such was all she could do, at that moment, with the lucidity Tufty Riquet had given her.

In his turn, he looked at her sadly.

"Madame,"[4] he said, "it's plain to see that you find me even more repulsive than the first time you laid eyes on me; when I gave you your mind I sealed my fate. You are still free, and you have the choice to marry me or go back to what you were; I will either return you to your father as I found you or I will make you the queen of this realm. I am the king of the gnomes, and you will be queen; if you are willing to forgive me my face, and to sacrifice the pleasure of your eyes, every other pleasure will be granted you in abundance. I own all the treasures that lie beneath the earth, and they will be yours; anyone who can be unhappy with money and a fine mind deserves it. I fear you might think yourself too good for me, though perhaps not for my riches. If you cannot bring yourself to accept me along with my wealth, then

---

4. Though today "madame" would be used only to address a married woman, in the seventeenth century, it was a suitable address for any noblewoman, married or not.

you need only say the word, and I will take you far away, for here I want nothing that troubles my happiness. You have two days to acquaint yourself with this place, and to decide your fate and my own."

Tufty Riquet took his leave after leading her to a magnificent apartment, where she was attended by gnomes of her own sex, whose ugliness she found less dire than the men's. They served her a meal that lacked nothing she could wish for, apart from good company. Afterward she went to the theater, where she found the actors so hideous she could take no interest in the story. That evening they held a ball in her honor, but she felt no desire to make herself agreeable.[5] In short, she was gripped by an unconquerable disgust, and would not have hesitated to tell Tufty Riquet he could keep his wealth and his pleasures and be done with him, were she not discouraged by the threat of finding herself once more an idiot.

She would gladly have sunk back into her stupidity to spare herself marriage to a man she loathed, except that she had a lover, and to return to her old self would be to lose him in the cruelest fashion. But of course she would be lost to him in any case, as soon as she married the gnome. Never could she see Arada, nor speak to him, nor even send news to him; at that very moment, he

---

5. The gnomes are performing the same courtesies and entertainment that would have been customary at Louis XIV's court.

might well have been suspecting her of infidelity. Thus, she would belong to a husband who, taking from her what she loved, would always be hateful to her even if he were handsome—but no, to make matters worse he was a horror. And so she found the choice exceedingly difficult to make.

The two days went by, and she was as uncertain as ever; she told the gnome she could not come to a decision.

"Then you have decided against me," he told her, "and so I will make you once again what you were, what you do not dare choose for yourself."

She trembled; the idea of losing her lover by the disdain he would feel for her stung her so sharply that she abandoned the fight.

"Well," she said to the gnome, "you have settled the question, and I must be yours."

Tufty Riquet did not quibble over the reasons; he married her, and from that marriage Mama's mind improved all the more, but her sadness grew along with her wit. She was horrified to have given herself to a monster, and she continually wondered how she could bear to spend another moment by his side.

The gnome did not fail to note his wife's hatred, and it hurt him, even if he prided himself on the strength of his will. Her aversion was a never-ending rebuke of his ugliness; it made him hate women, marriage, and the curiosity that had driven him out of the place he called home. He often left Mama alone, and since she had no other pastime than thinking, she resolved that she had to convince Arada by his own eyes that she was not faithless. He could come to this place, since she had; at the very least, she had to be able to tell him what had become of her, and explain her absence by showing him the gnome who had abducted her, the sight of whom would be assurance enough of her fidelity. Nothing is impossible for a clever woman in love. She won over one of the gnomes, who took word of her to Arada. Happily, the days of faithful lovers had not yet come to an end; he was despairing that Mama had forgotten him, but he felt no bitterness toward her. No insulting suspicion ever entered his mind; he was lost in lamentations, he was dying, but he never conceived a single thought that might offend his mistress, and never sought to forget his love for her. Tormented as he was by those emotions, it should come as no surprise that he no sooner learned where Mama was, and heard that she did not forbid him to come, than he ran straight off to find her, thinking nothing of the danger.

He entered the subterranean world where Mama was living, he saw her, he threw himself at her feet. She answered with words even more loving than they were wise. He obtained her permission to leave his world behind to come and live under the earth, and she did not give it readily, even though she had no other wish than to see him do just that.

Little by little Mama's good spirits returned, and so her beauty grew even more perfect, but the gnome was alarmed: he was too sharp-witted, and he knew too well the disgust he inspired in Mama, to believe that her sorrows had eased simply because she had grown used to the sight of him.[6] Mama was imprudent enough to dress in her finest clothes; he knew himself too well to think he was worthy of it. He racked his brains for some explanation, and finally concluded that there was a handsome man hiding somewhere in his palace; there was no need to search any further. He devised a vengeance more refined than simply dispatching his rival. He summoned Mama.

"I do not waste my time in complaints and reproaches," he told her. "I leave such things to men. When I gave you your mind, I was hoping it might bring me happiness. You have used it against me, but I cannot take it away from you, for you have duly submitted to the law that was imposed on you. Nonetheless, while you have not broken our pact, you have failed to observe it to the fullest. Let us share the chagrin: you will be intelligent by night, for I want no part of a stupid wife; but by day you will belong to whomever you please."

---

6. A common literary trope throughout medieval and early modern French literature suggests that when a woman becomes inexplicably more beautiful, it is a sign that she is cheating on her husband.

At that moment Mama felt her thoughts growing ever dimmer, and soon she felt not even that. Her intelligence reawoke only at night. She reflected on her sad lot; she wept; she could find the strength neither to comfort herself nor to seek the remedies that her mind might offer her.

The next night, she noticed that her husband was sound asleep; under his nose she put an herb that deepened his slumber and would keep him asleep for as long as she wished. She rose from their bed to escape the object of her hatred. Led onward by her reveries, she walked toward Arada's lodgings, not to seek him, but fondly musing that he might perhaps be seeking her. She found him on a garden path where they often met to talk, and where he was imploring all of nature to bring her to him. Mama told him of her sorrows, which were lightened by the pleasure she took in recounting them.

The next night, though they'd named no place or time, they once again found each other on that same path, and those tacit rendezvous went on for so long that their exile served only to let them taste a new happiness. Mama's love and ingenuity furnished her with a thousand expedients to make herself pleasing, and to make Arada forget that she lacked all intelligence half of the time.

When the lovers sensed that dawn was near, Mama went and woke the gnome, carefully taking the soporific away as soon as she was beside him. Day broke and she became an imbecile again—but she spent the day sleeping.

No happiness lasts forever; the leaves that brought sleep also brought snoring. A servant gnome who was neither fully asleep nor entirely awake feared that his master was in distress; he ran to him, saw the herbs that someone had placed under his nose, and snatched them away in the belief that they were disturbing him, a gesture that made three lives unhappy at once. The gnome saw that he was alone; beside himself with rage, he stormed out in search of his wife. Chance or bad luck led him to the spot where the two lovers were swearing their undying love. He said nothing, but he touched the lover with a stick that gave him a face like his own, and once he had changed places with him several times Mama could no longer make out which was which. She saw not one but two husbands, and never knew to which she might recount her sorrows, for fear that she might mistake the one she hated for the one she loved. But perhaps this was no great loss: lovers always become husbands in the end.

Catherine Durand

(c. 1650–?)

Our knowledge of Catherine's Durand's life is extremely limited. Her date of birth is unknown, and her date of death is difficult to verify. There is also conflicting information about whether Durand is her maiden or married name (Béda-cier being the other alternative; in all of her writings, she is referred to as Catherine Durand). Here is what is generally known: she came from a bourgeois family, and she wrote novels, three fairy tales, and a collection of proverbs. Her first fairy tale, "Histoire de la fée Lubantine" ("Story of the Fairy Lubantine"), appears in her 1699 novel *La comtesse de Mortane* (*The Countess of Mortane*). "Le prodige d'amour" ("A Miracle of Love") appears together with "L'origine des fées" ("The Origin of Fairies") in *Les petits soupers de l'esté 1699* (*The Little Suppers of 1699*). She was also presented with an award by the Académie Française in 1701, which suggests that she and her work were known in her own time.

Though less obviously so than Catherine Bernard's tale, this tale is a rewriting of the "Riquet à la houppe" story made famous by Perrault and Bernard. Durand's narrator, like Bernard's, is skeptical of love. In this story, the male charac-ter, Brutalis, is beautiful but stupid, and his behavior makes it clear that *esprit* extends to both intelligence and politeness. As Brutalis falls in love, his mannerisms and speeches are in-creasingly smart, witty, and thoughtful. Another twist in this version of the story is the creation of a fairy who has definite faults: she is coquettish, blinded by her ego, and unable to work the kind of miracle that she seeks when it comes to love. This fairy tale is the least well-known of the ones in this volume; by placing it together with Bernard's "Riquet" tale, we hope to inspire more comparisons and analyses of the "Riquet" trope.

Further Reading

Gethner, Perry. "Playful Wit in Salon Games: The Comedy Proverbs of Catherine Durand." *L'esprit en France au XVIIe siècle*, edited by François Lagarde, Papers on French Seventeenth-Century Literature, 1997, pp. 225–30.

Jasmin, Nadine. "Sophistication and Modernization of the Fairy Tale, 1690–1709." Translated and adapted by Sophie Raynard. *The Teller's Tale: Lives of the Classic Fairy-Tale Writers*, edited by Raynard, State U of New York P, 2013, pp. 41–46.

Seifert, Lewis C. "Durand, Catherine." *The Oxford Companion to Fairy Tales*, edited by Jack Zipes, Oxford UP, 2000, p. 143.

A Miracle of Love

Once there was a king whose wife met her end soon after she had borne him a son—a son of such exceptional beauty and vigor that the widower, who was not a young man, resolved not to remarry but to devote all his attention to his wonderful child. Until the boy learned to speak, the king was perfectly happy with his plan, but once the child began to say a few words, it was painfully clear that he was incapable of putting even one of them in the right place. At first the king thought this nothing more than an endearing childish quirk, and he delighted in the sweet nonsense his son spoke, but soon he began to worry: the young prince seemed so dull-witted that he was unable to find any interest or pleasure in the world around him. The innate curiosity of children, the endless questions that nature inspires in them and from which they so quickly learn, the boundless energy they derive from their youthful blood: in this boy all of that was dead. His face was charming, his figure flawless, but there was no soul animating that beautiful body, and so his father began to find his presence almost unbearable.

Sluggish, obtuse, and cheerless, the boy could not profit from the many tutors[1] he was given—for the king spared no expense on him, not so much because he thought it might help as because he was determined to do his fatherly duty. He had summoned all the world's most gifted teachers, in hopes that they might clear the tangles from his son's unkempt mind, but in vain: before long they came to him and with one voice announced that they had drawn on all their skill and knowledge to educate the prince, but they saw no good that could come from schooling him further, and so they sought the king's permission to go home.

The king could only agree. The prince, who had come to be called Brutalis, was then seventeen, an age at which even the crudest soul has begun to grow and take shape, but he was still mired in stupidity, and his physical beauty made his witlessness all the more insufferable. His father saw no solution but to dismiss the teachers, richly rewarded for their labors, and to find Brutalis a wife, hoping to bring himself some consolation by way of a grandson.

Finding a wife for Brutalis was no easy task. The neighboring kings had all learned of his monstrous idiocy, and they refused to burden their daughters with such a hus-

---

1. Noble young men were classically trained by tutors or *maîtres* ("masters") in all the liberal arts.

band. Worse yet, when Brutalis was brought before the kingdom's most beautiful women he only stared at them blankly. Asked if he found them beautiful, he answered, "I don't know about beautiful," then went off to the royal stables for a horse and rode out to hunt for the rest of the day.

Hunting was the one thing he liked, and even that he did with no grace. He was a strong, hearty youth, and a very able horseman, but he sat on his steed with so vacant an air that anyone who watched him ride by could see at a glance that he never had a thought in his head as others do.

One day, after a few hours' hunt, he called for a halt and dismounted to rest on the moss at the foot of a stout oak tree in a gloriously beautiful forest. But rather than lean back against the trunk he slumped forward with his chin against his chest, looking so imbecilic that one of his good fellow hunters had the idea of wrapping a flame-colored ribbon around his neck to keep him sitting upright, bound to the tree. Now that his position was no longer up to him, he looked a very elegant young man, with his lush blond hair fluttering in the wind and falling over his shoulders in a thousand thick curls that blended in with the ribbon and covered the bark where he was tied to the trunk. His good companion found him so handsome that he secretly mourned, lamenting the lot of a prince who could have been perfect if Nature had only consented to complete her work. Lost in these meditations, he wandered off into the woods, just as the other hunters silently drifted away, having nothing to say to a prince who could feel neither boredom nor pleasure.

Not far from that forest lived a fairy by the name of Mademoiselle Coquette, quite young, very pretty, neither immune to passion nor strict in her morals, with a keen eye for handsome young men. Her habit, when she was aggrieved by her latest lover's faithlessness, was to take her troubles out for a stroll in the solitude of nature, which is how she happened onto the very spot I just told you of, and found Brutalis resting. She first glimpsed him from behind, her gaze drawn by that abundance of beautiful hair and the prince's regal attire. All of this seemed to promise an adventure, and she made ready to pursue it, for she was a woman less inclined to dwell on her sorrows than to seek some way to shake them off. She consulted her pocket mirror, touched up her rouge, put on a few *mouches*,[2] and dried her tears, leaving just a few to keep the shine in her eyes.

Thus assured of her comeliness, she strolled past the prince. Any other man would at least have taken pleasure in gazing on her, with her nymph-like garb and her fetching manner, but Brutalis scarcely gave her a glance.

---

2. A *mouche* is, in this case, a tiny, decorative shape cut from black taffeta that ladies applied to their faces ("Mouche").

Mademoiselle Coquette concluded that he must be in the throes of some hopeless passion, or perhaps downcast after a tragic misfortune.

"What might be troubling you?" she asked as she sat down beside him. "How can this be, a man as fine as you so lost in sorrow?"

"I don't know what you mean," Brutalis answered, his gaze still fixed on the ground.

The bold fairy was greatly surprised by the tone in which he spoke those few words. "But why are you tied up like this?" she asked. "If you like, I can help you with that, for a start."

"Oh," he said, "they'll untie me when I get back on my horse."

"Yes, I imagine they will," she answered, astonished at such absolute resignation, and unable to hold back a laugh. "I don't suppose they'll pull up the oak and set it behind you."

"I don't know," the prince said again.

After such an exchange, you may well imagine that Mademoiselle Coquette needed no great finesse to grasp what manner of man she was dealing with. "But who are you?" she asked him.

"The son of the king," he answered.

Hearing those words, she remembered the stories she'd heard of the young prince; convinced that her charms might stir his emotions if not his intelligence, she said to him some very pretty things that he did not understand and did not even try to answer. Nevertheless, a lady likes to flatter herself, and when she saw the other hunters returning she withdrew, feeling a new passion and at least a glimmer of hope.

Back in her palace, she had her servants draw a bath laced with a thousand beauty-heightening concoctions and ordered them to bring several gowns, some very grand, others simply alluring, and to assemble a magnificent livery. This was soon done, and so one fine day, telling no one where she was bound, she set off in a display of splendor that surprised and puzzled all her court. The sylphs of the wood were always ready to obey her every command; they could have transported her through the air had she so wished, and she had a thousand other means of quick and effortless travel, but this seemed something more than a simple journey she was embarking on: it seemed almost a triumphal procession.

She stood alone on a chariot made of pearls, with a single giant ruby for a floor, majestically drawn by eight ruby-draped blue elephants; on each sat a beautiful girl, one playing the lute, another the theorbo,[3] and so on, every instrument sounding out in perfect harmony as the cortège advanced.

---

3. A theorbo is a type of bass lute.

Two hundred guards superbly outfitted in the Moorish fashion,[4] as spirited as the Moors of Granada, sat astride horses as noble as Bucephalus.[5] Her pages and escort were similarly attired, and the luggage-bearing elephants were covered in draperies worth a king's ransom.

Mademoiselle Coquette did not have to tell them where she wanted to go. She had enchanted the elephants pulling her chariot, and they took her straight to the kingdom of Paraminofara, the domain of Brutalis's father. Arriving in the capital city, she made it clear to her escort that she did not want to appear under her true name; curious onlookers were thus told that she was Princess Azindara, passing through on a long voyage. The king was informed, and assured that nothing so lovely had ever been seen in his land. He hurried out to greet the great princess, and they exchanged many a gracious compliment. Already the good king loved Princess Azindara as if she were his own daughter; learning that she had no husband, he passionately hoped that she might not spurn his son, though he knew that was likely

---

4. A Moor is "a member of a people of mixed Arab and Berber ancestry inhabiting ancient Mauretania in North Africa and conquering Spain in the 8th century A.D." ("Moor"). By the time of these tales (in what we might today consider a textbook example of Orientalism), Moorish culture had become synonymous in France with splendor and elegance; no doubt for that reason, the fairies of these stories habitually surround themselves with Moorish servants, guards, and so on.

5. Bucephalus was Alexander the Great's favorite horse, celebrated in antiquity for its strength, beauty, and loyalty.

a hopeless dream unless the princess was a very charita-
ble woman.

Her mind firmly fixed on one goal, Mademoiselle Coquette asked the king to tell her of his family. He dis-
solved into tears and answered that he had only a son.
"Well," said she, "why should that be a cause for despair,
if he has merit?"

"Alas, my lady," he answered, "that is precisely my
sorrow: his outward appearance is pleasing, but he is
cursed with an idiocy that all the education I have given
him has not been able to overcome."

"Send for him," said Mademoiselle Coquette, "and I
will judge if he can be cured." Delighted by her eagerness, the king ordered one of his officers to tell Brutalis
he was wanted, and to dress him as if for the ball.

Soon he was brought in, adorned with all manner of
finery to bring out his beauty, but his gait was lumber-
ing, his head bowed, his eyes fixed on the ground. "Raise
your head, Prince," said the false Azindara, and for a moment he did. "But you must also raise your eyes," she
told him; he was docile enough to obey, but his stare was
vacant. The king despaired. He knew there was a reason
why Azindara was taking such an interest in his son, and
he would have given anything for the honor of bringing
her into his family. He told her so, in a few short words,
and her answer was all he could have hoped. "But," she
added, "he must give me some sign that he might one

day be like other men." The king respectfully wished her good luck and ordered several days of festivities in her honor.

Mademoiselle Coquette retired early, to ensure that she would be beautiful for the next evening's party. She was even lovelier than the day before, and every eye was drawn to her. The evening's first entertainment was a carousel,[6] at which all expected the prince to appear, since riding was the one thing he was fond of. But it is one thing to chase after a deer, and quite another to elegantly perform the many feats and exercises required by a carousel. His fine clothes and handsome face made him seem only more ridiculous—to everyone but Mademoiselle Coquette, that is, for her passion was visibly mounting, as were her hopes. She was firmly convinced that her eyes alone were enchanting enough to transform young Brutalis, and if so, then what glory would come to them both! How her tender, natural power would outshine that of her fellow fairies, who required all their arts to attract a man's love!

Nevertheless, she decided to use one trick of the fairy trade during the fireworks that concluded the day's entertainments. As everyone was eagerly awaiting the next display, a little rocket shot up in the air, weaving this way and

---

6. In this context, a carousel is a competition among horsemen, requiring them to perform various feats and challenges.

that as prettily as can be; but then, rather than the usual pop of gunpowder, it spoke the following words:

> The fates have decided Brutalis's fortune;
> Witty and brave he shall be;
> Among the finest folk he will shine bright,
> But Love alone can work that miracle.

The king listened to those words as if they were a decree from Jupiter himself; he looked at Coquette, seeing in her the tool Love might most likely use, then turned to Brutalis and asked, "My son, did you hear what that rocket just said?"

"I heard something," he answered, "but I don't know what it was."

"Can this be?" said Mademoiselle Coquette, biting her lip. "You were predicted a glorious future, and you weren't even listening?"

"I don't know what you're talking about," he said, then turned to look at the pretty girls in the fairy's entourage, though he said not a word to them. Thinking herself very shrewd, Mademoiselle Coquette concluded that the one sure way to win the Prince's heart would be to lure him to some solitary place where she was the only beauty to be seen, and where there was thus nothing to distract him.

Having devised this plan, she was eager to be away from the kingdom of Paraminofara, but she resolved to attend the next day's festivities, since there would be a ball, and as the finest dancer in all the land she might perhaps stir Brutalis's desire. The next evening, then, she appeared in a gown so laden with gemstones as to out-shine all the treasures of India. Next to her, all the other ladies seemed clumsy and ponderous; she had an easy grace about her that made the good king weep for joy. As for Brutalis, he blankly sang along with the violins, and although his voice was very soft he was an annoyance to everyone: for one thing he sang very badly, and for an-other he seemed to find no pleasure in any of this. He never once looked at Azindara, which pierced his father's heart like a dagger. Worse yet for the king, he soon found the fairy bidding him farewell. "I will be off now, my lord," she said, "not because my feelings have changed, but because sometimes there is more than one way to get what one wants, and I believe I have devised a fool-proof plan. But that means I must leave you, and should you soon find yourself without news of the prince for some time, do not be alarmed." Hearing these words, the king kissed her hand and beseeched her to remember her promise, for it was only his faith in her that kept him from dying at the very thought of her leaving.

Early the next day, Mademoiselle Coquette was mak-ing ready to set off when the king, who had given orders that he be alerted when that fateful hour sounded, came to remind her of her promises. She repeated them once more; then, after a fond embrace, she climbed onto her chariot and left just as she had come. Once she was back in her palace, her servants devoted three full days to her recovery from the strains and exhaustions of travel; as soon as she felt herself again, she ordered a sylph to transport her to the forest where she had first laid eyes on Brutalis.

She knew she would not fail to find him there, and so she did, out for a hunt as usual. Caught up in the excitement of the chase, he had ridden far ahead of the grooms, but his horse soon lost a shoe, so he leapt to the ground to wait for the others. He would soon have seen them had he not found himself being drawn into the woods by an invisible, inescapable force. He cried out, but no one came; not even his horse had followed him. Whose work could this have been, if not Mademoiselle Coquette's? She emerged from behind a bush, gently took his hand, and sat down beside him. "Are you very angry that I took you away from your hunting to bring you here?" she asked.

"Why will you not let me see the deer at bay? That's a deer at her most beautiful!" he answered.

"But," said Coquette, "I'm more beautiful than any deer, and if what you like to see is her tears, then soon you shall see me weep as much as any deer ever did, if you refuse to look at me, and if your heart should reject me."

All through this little admission of love, Brutalis was gazing at a magpie in a tree above the fairy, and he had no other thought in his mind. "Come now, look at me," she said. "It's not polite to stare into the distance when you're being spoken to." The poor prince obeyed, and he let out an innocent laugh, displaying two perfect rows of pearls.

Dismayed at his imbecility, Coquette began to lose hope. "Oh! A lot of good this has done me!" she cried. "Would Love even bother to fire an arrow at so undeserving a heart? And would anything more come of it than with a wild animal?"

"What's that you say?" Brutalis asked, since hunting was his one passion. "I thought I heard something about an animal."

"You did," she said. "Will you never tired of bearing that name of yours, and will you never have a mind to match your beauty?"

"I don't know what you mean," he answered, "but I'd rather be hunting."

Mademoiselle Coquette, on the other hand, had no wish to linger in those verdant woods; she ordered a sylph to transport her and Brutalis to a little palace she'd built for her amorous projects. They were there in a trice. "Well!" Mademoiselle Coquette asked Brutalis once the sylph set them down, "how did you like being carried through the air?"

"I'd rather be on my horse," he answered, "because then I'd be hunting."

"Have you really forgotten you've seen me before?" asked Coquette.

"I don't know if I have," he replied.

Mademoiselle Coquette took Brutalis by the hand and tried to interest him in the curiosities of her palace. The outer walls were concealed behind a luxuriant growth of honeysuckle and jasmine, and the roof was a terrace ringed with a railing of those same flowers. Nearby there were basins, two delightful little bowling greens,[7] and a deeply shaded wood in the form of a labyrinth, filled with little fountains whose coolness offered pleasant relief from the heat of the noonday sun. Each of her wonderful gardens offered a different view, all of them pleasantly varied; the celebrated Gardens of Semiramis[8] might have been larger, but they could not rival the delights of this one. Inside, every element of the décor was designed to inspire love: little porcelain-tiled salons always graced with fresh flowers, furniture upholstered in multicolored silk, beds ornamented with garlands of orange flowers held up by cupids, mirrors that made everything they reflected more perfect than in nature,

---

7. Technically, a bowling green is an area of well-trimmed grass, used for the game of lawn bowls, a common feature of fine English houses; the fashion for bowling greens spread to France, where they underwent a change of name—*boulingrin*—and of purpose, becoming strictly ornamental.

8. The hanging gardens of Babylon (also known as the Gardens of Semiramis) were one of the seven wonders of the ancient world.

aviaries full of birds whose songs immediately touched the heart. These and a thousand other delights conceived by the ingenious Mademoiselle Coquette would inevitably have stirred up at least some sentiment in anyone other than Brutalis, but after he had visited the entire palace—and not by choice—he dropped into an armchair and began to whistle, right there in front of the fairy, without so much as a glance in her direction.

This was all nearly more trying than she could endure, but she was determined to see her undertaking through to the end, not to mention that her heart was genuinely captivated. A meal was served, its every dish finer than ambrosia; the nectar of the gods could not begin to compare with the wine that accompanied it. The prince had a healthy appetite; he sat right down at the table and ate prodigiously. Coquette did what she could to engage him. She asked if he was unhappy to be with her, and if he was perhaps impatient to see his father again.

"Oh! well," he answered, "if I had a horse, I'd go right off and join him."

"Please," she replied, "don't do that, stay here with me for a while. I want to try to wake up your mind."

"Well, go ahead," he said. It was a great feat if she managed to draw two or three words out of him in an evening.

Several days went by. Coquette dressed him in sumptuous clothes, curled his long hair, adorned his face with *mouches*; he was as beautiful as Love itself, but his stupidity was still without equal. The fairy did everything that could possibly be done to make herself beautiful and him happy. She sang him tender love songs. Her Moorish servant women (she had taken care to exclude all the others)[9] danced ballets for him, their every step and movement alluring enough to stir emotion in a stone, but all these pleasures were wasted on him, and all her tender affections were expended for nothing. When she asked if he was bored, he answered with a yawn, "No, I'm not bored, but I'd rather be hunting." Shoulders sagging, Mademoiselle Coquette made no reply.

She often led him to the labyrinth I spoke of earlier, and urged him to admire its beauties. "Very nice," he said, "but what's it for?"

"For?" the fairy shot back. "Well, to begin with it's a pleasure for the eyes, but if you love me there is another use it could be put to, something I shouldn't speak of."

"I don't mind you," he answered, "but I don't like you more here than I would anywhere else."

"Oh, Prince," she said, "if you knew what love is, and if love for me had wounded your heart, you would be

---

9. Coquette seems to assume that a Moorish woman can pose no threat to her amorous designs—a surprising supposition, but one that fits with the fetishization of blondness that is so evident throughout these stories.

only too happy to be in a lonely place, where no one can see or hear."

It was far beyond Brutalis's capacities to make out the passion that shone through her words. "Oh!" he said, "I don't want to be wounded, and I like you as much when you're with your serving girls as when you're here by yourself." Then he stood up to look out at the view, or rather to look at nothing at all. Often Mademoiselle Coquette would stay behind in the woods and weep upon hearing an answer like that, but many times she followed after him, unwilling to abandon her hopes.

One day Brutalis was vacantly staring at a beautiful meadow and the brook that ran through it when he spied a shepherdess tending her little flock; her air was noble, and she seemed new to this task. Brutalis turned to Coquette and said, "Make that shepherdess come closer, I'd like to see her."

"What?" Coquette answered. "Do you find her prettier than me?"

"How should I know?" he said. "You're all I ever see, and this will make a change."

"Cruel man!" the fairy answered. "Will you never stop torturing me?"

"All right then," he interrupted, "I'll call her." And he bellowed at the shepherdess to come near, in the same tone he used when he was hunting and his dogs lost the scent. Surprised, the shepherdess turned around, revealing a charming face, as best it could be judged from such a distance. Seeing that it was a man calling her, she summoned her flock and led them away. "Oh!" said the prince, "she's very proud. Still, I'd like to see her again, because she looked pretty."

There was an innocence about Brutalis that often forced the fairy to smile; such was the case at this moment, even though jealousy was needling her cruelly. She bade him join her in her apartments, where she endeavored to make him forget the shepherdess with a thousand sweet words and a thousand tender caresses, and although that evening he seemed more pensive than usual, he spoke as many foolish words as he ever did.

Early the next day he returned to the garden, where he did not fail to see the shepherdess. Even a modest woman is happy to be looked at if she is beautiful, so he was able to gaze on her as long as he liked, and she made no move to flee as she had the day before. He gave her a moderately correct bow, and she answered with a very elegant curtsey; had he not heard the footsteps of Mademoiselle Coquette's maidservants, who had set out to look for him, he could have gone on for some time delighting in the sight of the shepherdess. The day went by with no other occasion to return to the spot that was fast becoming so dear to him. He had enough presence of mind to show no sign of impatience, but he could think of nothing but going back and seeing the sweet shepherdess again the next day.

He rose even earlier than the day before and hurried off to the usual spot, where he soon saw the shepherdess come along, singing a pastoral song in a delicate voice that stirred him to the core. He even remembered a song someone had once tried to teach him, and since he had a fine voice, he sang it prettily. No more did he roughly summon the shepherdess; rather, he gave her a little wave inviting her to approach. She took a few steps forward; pretending to busy herself petting her dog, she showed the young prince a smiling, enchanting face. He looked at her with a pleasure and a yearning that were beginning to free his gaze from the dullness and dimness that once hid its beauty. He was wrenched from that delectable occupation only by the arrival of Mademoiselle Coquette: she had risen not long after him, and having vainly sent her servants to look for him all over the palace, she was coming to see if he might be in the garden. Fortunately for him, he'd heard her approach, and he had time to wave the shepherdess away. He left that fateful place, and used the intelligence love had already given him to prevent the fairy from suspecting the pleasure he had just felt. To all appearances, he was just as mindless as ever, and when later that day Coquette tried out her charms on him again, her only reward was another string of infuriating inanities.

The next day he returned once again to the place of his delight, and when he spied the shepherdess there even earlier than the day before he found in himself all the love that he needed to untangle the knots in his mind. For her part, the shepherdess did more than simply allow herself to be looked at; now and then she turned her beautiful eyes toward the prince, and her gaze filled him with hope.

Nothing frees the mind like love, on that point everyone agrees: it civilizes the coarsest brute. Even the roughest heart is soon polished smooth when it is placed in hands of an artisan as skillful as love, and the prince more than proved the truth of that rule. For one thing, his manner became gentler, thanks to the feelings the shepherdess had inspired in him; for another, as his passion swelled his mind began to shine with a brilliant light. In his eagerness to please his beloved, to earn her admiration, all the instruction his teachers had given him came flooding back from the depths of his memory, miraculously endowing him with an eloquence that astonished everyone who had seen him just the day before. More than that: he cultivated, so to speak, the learnings that everyone believed had been planted in sterile soil, and everything about him was splendid and noble.

We last saw the prince gazing on his mistress, in the first moments of the effects I have just briefly detailed; realizing that the fairy would soon come looking for him, and fully understanding her powers, he was wise enough to tear himself away from a place that each day brought him new delights. He went off to find Mademoiselle Coquette, and as he gave her a bow more creditable than usual he could not stop a few lucid words from escaping his lips. Fearing he might inspire hope or suspicion in that redoubtable fairy, he took care to answer her questions as foolishly as he could, or better yet to say nothing at all.

He went so far as to claim he was ill so that he could retire to his rooms. Already the brainless Brutalis had learned to lie and to pretend—and more than that, to think, seeking some way of seeing his shepherdess again, which was a thorny problem indeed. He could not leave the palace without the fairy at his side; although it was not a sure solution, then, he took the chance of writing the following note:

> I am dying of impatience to see you and talk to you, but I can only leave this palace in the company of the fairy Coquette, who is holding me prisoner, and I cannot see how I might come to you. But if tomorrow you would do me the great kindness of leading your flock further along, into the woods, then you may find me there. It will be only a little longer walk for you, and by your indulgence you will make me the happiest of all men.

On finishing this letter, the besotted prince went to bed, but he slept very little, and indeed not at all until he had come up with a plan for conveying his note to the shepherdess. When he awoke, he picked up a bow, slipped the letter through the feathers of an arrow, and very deftly—for he was an excellent marksman—shot it so that it would fall to earth just a few feet away from the shepherdess. She had no doubt that the paper was intended for her. Out of discretion and modesty, she sat down before she picked it up; she called to one of her ewes, sang a song, petted her dog, then finally took up the paper and read the words you have just seen. She kept her eyes fixed on the grass, almost not daring to look up, but in the end she could not help herself: she turned toward the prince and gave him a little nod to signify that she would accede to his wish. He was plunged into a transport of joy, and for the rest of the day, no matter how hard he tried to maintain his usual blank expression, his shining eyes spoke for his silent tongue. Thinking herself clearly very desirable— and rightly so—Mademoiselle Coquette exulted in the progress she believed she was making in young Brutalis's heart. He needed to have her on his side for the success of his plan, so he did not disabuse her of her happy misunderstanding, and uttered a few words that convinced her of the power of her beauty. That evening, more infatuated than ever, she asked the prince what sort of entertainment might please him, and he asked her to take him out hunting. She was only too happy to offer him that pleasure, which was put off no further than the very next day.

Mademoiselle Coquette had her maidservants curl and powder her light chestnut hair, then donned a diamond-embroidered hunting outfit and mounted a superb dapple-gray horse with a flame-colored mane. She looked every inch like Bradamante.[10] Brutalis too was magnificently attired, as were the rest of the hunting party, who saw the gleam in the prince's eyes and thought it must have been caused by the sight of a fine pack of hounds, every one of which deserved a panegyric[11] to itself.

Coquette was an excellent horsewoman, for it was in her power to be whatever she pleased. She kept her horse trotting just next to Brutalis's. He was so handsome that day that she found an inexpressible happiness in seeing him and speaking to him, and she was more determined than ever to win him. The deer that was released for the hunt did not survive long, and there were still hours of daylight to go when they witnessed the kill. Coquette beckoned Brutalis to ride some distance away, where she promised he would see something very beautiful. Alas! She had no idea how right she was; fate makes dupes of the cleverest of us. Brutalis readily agreed, hoping he might meet his shepherdess, and turned into the woods with Mademoiselle Coquette. She knew all manner of secret paths, and she chose a glade where a silvery spring poured in a gentle murmur from a large stone and flowed

---

10. Bradamante: a heroine and knight in Ludovico Ariosto's epic poem *Orlando furioso*, first published in 1516.

11. A panegyric is a formal writing or oration in elaborate praise of someone or something.

on between mossy banks. She jumped down from her horse, inviting the prince to do the same, and they sat by the side of the stream.

"Well!" she said, pulling the prince closer and laying her head on his knees. "What are you thinking, here in this quiet place? Do you feel something stirring inside you?"

"I'm thinking," answered Brutalis, looking at her with eyes that seemed clearer than usual, "that this is a very nice sort of solitude, and I feel happier here than I might somewhere elsewhere."

"Ah!" cried the fairy, who found some sense in these words and thought herself the cause of that miracle, "no more will you bear the disagreeable name of Brutalis; henceforth you will be the beautiful Polidamour!"[12] Gathering up the prince's thousand curls all around his brow, she went on, "And when we are married you will know a happiness that never ends!"

Polidamour was thinking of something entirely different as Coquette reveled in her delusion. Chance—or more precisely the blind god who sees so clearly when he wants to—had led the shepherdess past the rock and its spring, and he had seen her walk past. His ardent love and his yearning to talk to her would not let him sit idly by; he had to seize the moment. He leapt to his feet and told the fairy he wanted to go off for a look around.

---

12. Literally, *poli d'amour* would mean "polished by love."

The fairy was stunned by his manner. She saw him walk away with a vigorous, self-assured gait; never had he seemed so worthy of love, and never did she have better reason to fear she might lose him. She began to suspect that Love had some terrible tribulation in store for her, and as she sat lost in thought the prince had more than enough time to see his plan through. But soon she could restrain her impatience no longer, and she tremblingly hurried off to look for him. Imagine her surprise when she saw him kneeling before the shepherdess she had glimpsed from the terrace! Her despair was beyond words, and her first thought was to assail the thankless prince with a thousand stinging rebukes. But a second thought stopped her: she wanted to see how all this ended, and to give her jealousy time to inflame her fury.

Hidden behind a bush, she could see and hear everything, and everything she saw and heard soon plunged her into the depths of misery. The shepherdess was in the very flower of youth and the unsullied beauty that comes with it: her ash-blond curls, mingled with pomegranate flowers, gave her the very special glow that only the fair-haired possess. Her eyes, of indefinable color, shot tender, lively glances through her long, black lashes. Her skin was dazzlingly white; her red, bowed lips wore a gracious smile that created a thousand little delights around her mouth. Her face was almost round, and a little cleft in her chin gave her a proud, delicate air. Her slightly upturned nose had a youthful look that seemed bound to stay with it for years to come; her bust was shaped by the Graces themselves. Poor Coquette had all too many occasions to gaze on her white, delicate hands, for the shepherdess used them to conceal every blush brought to her lovely face by the prince's sweet words and breathtaking beauty.

Her gown was of fine silk, ornamented with lace; a length of floral fabric served as her belt, and although she was sitting her waist seemed so slender and lithe that after closely examining her figure and all the other wonders of her beauty Mademoiselle Coquette could only cry out in despair, "O merciless heavens! What a rival you have given me!"

The lovers were too lost in their conversation to hear the fairy's wail. Kneeling at the shepherdess's feet, Polidamour thanked her for consenting to venture into this forest; his gratitude gave him a lovably boyish air. Not looking him in the eye, she answered that she would just as soon lead her flock to the forest as to the meadow.

"Oh!" interrupted the lovestruck prince, "do not recant an innocent favor that makes me the happiest of men. We have no time to waste on ceremony. I love you, and there is nothing I will not do to prove it. I ask only that you tell me if your heart is in any way moved by me and my love for you."

"Alas!" she answered, blushing, "I fear you might think less of me if I answered with a confession, however happy you might be to hear it. If you do indeed love me, you might perhaps think me too forward. But you say we have no time to lose, and I would be distraught if you were to go away without having been told that, owing to feelings over which I have no control . . ." The young shepherdess stopped there, and handsome Polidamour cried out in boundless joy, "Wonderful feelings! Charming words! I only wish I could die here at your feet to give you the thanks that I owe you."

But Mademoiselle Coquette could take no more, and could not hold herself back; indeed, many of her servants were astonished that she had waited so long. She burst out from behind the bush, and in a thundering voice asked the prince who had taught him so well. He rose to his feet and helped his shepherdess do the same.

"My lady," he said to Coquette, "it was Love that worked this wonder; you predicted it yourself. I am sorry he did not work his magic through you,"—and here the prince broke into a smile—"but he is a capricious sort, who makes me spurn a great fairy's attentions and worship a simple shepherdess as fervently as I would the most glorious deity."

The cavalier tone of the prince's words so clearly showed Mademoiselle Coquette the superiority of the shepherdess's charms that she bristled with rage. Glowering furiously at her rival all the while, she answered Polidamour, "You have not progressed as far as you think.

Your eloquence may well flag one day; or it may discover a new target. You speak as well as any other man, and better, but do not expect me to sit by and despair. Fear my righteous wrath, or else stop loving an insignificant shepherdess, who will soon learn if it is wise for one such as her to vex a fairy."

The timorous shepherdess, whose name was Brillante, had been raised to fear these formidable women whose worst vices were never criticized. She fell to her knees in a flood of tears and begged forgiveness for the wrong she had innocently done.

"Come now," answered Coquette, "there is no such thing as an innocent rival." And as she spoke she seized Brillante by the arm and held her fast.

"My lady, where is your generosity of spirit?" said the prince. "You made a prediction, and your prediction has come true; that speaks highly of your wisdom. All the rest was the work of my shepherdess's eyes." He tried to pull his mistress from the fairy's menacing hands, but simple human strength was not enough. "Very well, then," he cried. "You may inflict any torment you like on this divine girl and me, but you will never force my heart to cast off its chains for others."

Those are terrible words for a woman in love, and they struck Coquette with full force. But she loved him still, and those stirred by that passion are not given to patience and moderation: their tempers grow even hotter. "You ingrate," she said to Polidamour, "I loved you, I told you so, and my only reward is to see an unworthy rival defeat me?" She broke into tears. "I bring you to a place where I believe I will find you less inflexible, only to find myself shamed and humiliated? Do not resist, lowly shepherdess: follow me, and mind you do not glance even once at your barbarous lover." That order was not obeyed; having fallen in love, Brillante had learned the art of concealing her gaze from a rival, and her eyes met Polidamour's again and again.

No sooner had Mademoiselle Coquette spoken, her eyes ablaze with anger, than there appeared a dark cave, guarded by two horrible Furies, who bore sweet Brillante away. The prince was as brave as he was loving, but he struggled in vain to pull her free. "Oh, cruel fate!" he cried. "No sooner have I tasted the sweetness of love than the one I adore is snatched away! There is nothing my reason can do for me, save inspire me to mourn my whole life through for the woman who rescued me from my mindlessness. No, my life will not be long, cruel woman," he added, speaking to Mademoiselle Coquette, "and your rage will soon lose the power to affect me. This blade will soon put an end to my many sorrows." And as he spoke these words, he drew his sword. Were it not for the fairy's power over the forces of the air, handsome Polidamour would have been a dead man; but three or four sylphs soon disarmed him and led him to his tormentor's palace.

What thoughts filled the prince's mind in that cruel confinement! No longer the dullard he had been, he keenly felt the bleakness of his plight. Mademoiselle Coquette treated him only too well; under the effect of Polidamour's newfound wit and her own jealousy, her passion had swelled beyond measure. She did all she could to sway him, and his rebuffs stung her but did not alter her feelings.

Finally he decided the only solution was to pretend to fall back into stupidity. At first she doubted him, but as time went by with no change she began to worry. She feared that her excessive affections had brought about a relapse; her tenderness overpowering her reason, she felt she must find some remedy for that ingrate she loved too much. But what a remedy! For there was only one, and a risky one it was: he had to be allowed to see Brillante. For some time she could not bring herself to attempt that experiment, but in the end she found the strength in her desire to come to the aid of her lover.

One question still bedeviled her: should she take him there herself, or should she entrust him to loyal emissaries who would faithfully tell her all that had transpired? The first way seemed surer, but also more painful: what could be worse than to see the eyes of a man one loves light up at the sight of another woman? That thought convinced her to place him in the hands of two sylphs, whose quick, subtle minds seemed well suited to such a use.

Mademoiselle Coquette had those two sylphs take the form of two fearsome tigers. They bound Polidamour up in chains of flowers, stronger than metal, then set off for the cave where young Brillante was imprisoned. Polidamour had heard their orders, and resolved to appeal to their compassion. Inspired by his sorrow, his eloquence soared to new heights, but he had not drawn one word from the taciturn tigers when they arrived at the cave's entrance. They ordered the two Furies to let the prince enter. All the signs seemed encouraging, and that horrid cavern— better suited to a savage beast than to a poor beautiful girl—seemed to him a delicious palace, where every happiness awaited him.

"So at long last I see you again," he said to the shepherdess, "and at long last I can freely tell you everything I feel for you."

Brillante was lying in a dark corner, on a bed of leaves she had made for herself, weeping perhaps as much at the absence of her lover as at her own captivity. She raised her beautiful eyes to him; deeply moved by this undreamt-of joy, she said, "It's you! What happy event could have brought you here to this place where none of the cruelties I endured have for one moment distracted me from my thoughts of you?" Their happy reunion soon led the two lovers to share their deepest secrets, which is one of the great pleasures of love.

The prince told her his story, and he found a sweet delight in thanking her for a passion whose intensity was in no way the opposite of reason: indeed, it had brought about the birth of his reason.

Brillante was no less eager to tell him about herself, which she did as follows: "My lord, allow me to justify the fondness you have come to feel for me: I am a princess, and my father is the king of the Île Galante.[13] The Île Galante is a most pleasant place: love stirs in us as soon as our minds begin to develop, but we believe that variety is, if not a virtue, at least so great a pleasure that it would be wrong to go through life without it.

"My father lives by that maxim, to the letter: there never was a more inconstant man than he. When I left the island, he had already dallied with every one of the beautiful women in his court, and was moving on to the ugly ones. He said he would sooner take up with ladies well past the age of nubile charms than live without variety. 'Is it not a laudable curiosity,' he said, 'to study all the many different

---

13. *Galant* is a favorite word of the late seventeenth and eighteenth centuries, with a rich multiplicity of meanings: courtly, alluring, elegant, flirtatious, and erotic, for example. The Île Galante, or Isle of Gallantry, will be evoked again in "The Pleasant Punishment," though without the implication of systematic infidelity.

ways of loving there are, to examine all the diversity of the
human character, to step back into centuries past so to
speak, by spending time with a venerable woman, and a
woman of rich experience?' None of that spoke to me in
any way; on the contrary, I was sure nothing could be
sweeter than to be bound to one person for all one's life.
Many princes from my father's kingdom courted and wor-
shipped me, but in vain: I was put off by their dangerous
sophistries, and since my heart was not made to be cruel,
I avoided the Île Galante's endless festivities whenever
I could.

"'Who knows?' I used to think as I walked alone in
the woods. 'Suppose someday one of those suitors stirred
something inside me—would it not be a curse to be
taken in by the charms of a philanderer who would soon
leave me for another?' It was then that I heard a nightingale[14] sing these words, as clearly as can be:

> Princess, the gods have willed it:
> You must leave this place at once.
> Accept the aid of an invisible hand,
> And feel the power your eyes exert
> On the heart of one who loves sincerely.
> You alone can give him a precious gift,

---

14. In Greek mythology, Philomela is turned into a nightingale after
being raped by her sister's husband, Tereus. Thus, there is a literary
tradition of associating the nightingale with sorrow.

He alone can give you a life of delight and
    tranquility.

"Deeply surprised by these words, I looked all around
me but saw only a faint mist. A moment later that mist had
slipped beneath my feet and carried me off to this land.
The gems adorning my robe afforded me the means to buy
a shepherdess's attire, and to live among the local villagers.
My hopes for the future kept me alive. As you see, my lord,
if I have justified your love for me by my story, my oracle
absolves me of all shame at my feelings for you. I cannot
doubt that you are the lover who is destined to make me
happy, and the gift I have given you is indeed precious. But
I only untangled the chaos that was encumbering your
thoughts; your reason and wit were always inside you,
needing only a spark to shine with all the fire they show
today. Love is a great teacher; it brought order to the
chaos of the entire vast universe, so how could it fail to
tame the chaos in a heart that was ready to submit to its
power?"

His soul filled with joy, Polidamour showered a thousand kisses on his beautiful princess's lovely hand. They
had both lost all awareness of their surroundings and forgotten the power of the fairy, but now one of the tigers
came to announce that the time had come for them to
part. They cried out in pain at that terrible command, and
their grief roused the sylph's mercy: "Come, take heart,"

he said with a smile, or as close as a tiger can come to a smile. "I want to serve as an ally in your love, for even in our airy empire we are no strangers to sentiment." He turned toward the princess: "I will deceive you no longer," he said, adopting the form of a handsome young man. "It was I who transported you here from the Île Galante, charged with overseeing your fate. Mademoiselle Coquette could not have made a worse choice for her servant! She has some power over us, but we can free ourselves of it whenever the fancy takes us." He called to the other tiger, who now took on the same form as he, so alike that they could not be told apart.

Conjuring solid forms from the air around them, they summoned up a very pretty little carriage, as the Furies stood by in silence, powerless to oppose them. "Now," said one of the sylphs, "let us complete our triumph and our deception, and inform Mademoiselle Coquette of your adventure." A porphyry[15] pyramid appeared from the ground, and on it the joyful spirits engraved the following words:

> In the future, take care whom you choose
> As agents for your vengeance,
> And forget these two lovers forever:
> Henceforth, the only sorrows they will know

---

15. Porphyry: a very hard type of marble.

Are the sorrows felt by loving hearts.

They will never lay eyes on you again,

For their happiness will be too complete.

With that the four of them set off together, and were very soon in the kingdom of Paraminofara. How profound was the king's joy on seeing his son transformed into the most charming of all men! The sylphs recounted the lovers' story down to the smallest detail, and the king, drinking in their words, was so furious at Mademoiselle Coquette—also, he learned from the sylphs, known as Azindara—that he forgot he had ever hoped to see her become Polidamour's wife. As for Brillante, he thought her a very fine match. One of the sylphs went off to ask her hand from her father, and came back with a favorable reply. The king of Paraminofara demanded only that upon the death of the king of the Île Galante the abuses that had corrupted that land would be banned forever.

The wedding festivities were magnificent. Second only to the bride and groom, the princes of the air were the stars of the gathering, and inspired love in more than one young woman eager for the glory of immortalizing a lover.[16] But the fickle sylphs went on their way as soon as they had won their immortality; not knowing whom

---

16. Legend had it that spirits of the four elements could become immortal if they gained the love of a mortal woman.

to complain to, their mistresses sought less agreeable but more reliable conquests.

As for Mademoiselle Coquette, she fell into an all-consuming rage on reading the pyramid's inscription, and took to her bed for some time. But soon a renewal of her hopes spurred her recovery, and—knowing she had the king of Paraminofara's favor, which she thought unshakable—she left for his court on a hippogriff, only to find the prince married and still in love with his wife. There was nothing she could do, and after many machinations and adventures of which she should have been ashamed, she had no choice but to return to her old palace, for the one I have told of here now existed only in the imaginary realms.

CHARLOTTE-ROSE CAUMONT DE LA FORCE

(c. 1650–1724)

Charlotte-Rose Caumont de La Force was born into a noble Protestant family that had been sympathetic to the Huguenots during the French Wars of Religion. She was related to Henriette-Julie de Castlenau, comtesse de Murat, on her mother's side. Like Catherine Bernard, she converted to Catholicism in 1686 after the revocation of the Edict of Nantes (1685). Unlike Bernard, however, La Force had a series of scandals and love affairs that were all the more publicized because of her status at court. She served as lady-in-waiting to Queen Marie-Thérèse, first wife of Louis XIV, and received a pension from the king. In 1687, she married the much younger Charles de Briou without the consent of his father. The marriage was annulled two years later. In 1697, a time that was marked by Louis XIV's desire to create a court whose members reflected only the most virtuous morals and behaviors, La Force lost the king's favor after being accused of possessing a pornographic novel and was exiled to a Benedictine convent in Gercy. Here, she wrote historical novels and her 1697 *Les contes des contes* (*The Tales of the Tales*). She also wrote poems that appeared in *Le Mercure galant*. After she was authorized to return to court in 1715 (after the death of Louis XIV), she lived quietly until her death in 1724.

La Force's *Les contes des contes* introduces new traits into the vogue of French literary tales. Though these tales appeared the same year as collections by Perrault and d'Aulnoy, they are distinct in style. They are not set in frame narratives like those of Marie-Catherine d'Aulnoy, Bernard, or Catherine Durand. The tales also stand out for their (relative) brevity and their diversity of messages about love, in contrast to the *contes* of Bernard and Murat, for example. La Force also rewrites other literary texts of many kinds: while "L'enchanteur" ("The Enchanter"), for example, is a retelling of the medieval *Perceval*, others focus on characters and episodes from Greek and Roman mythology.

"Vert et Bleu" ("Green and Blue") is one of the most unusual *contes* of this vogue of fairy tales. Though the characters follow the expected trajectory—conflict followed by union in marriage—they must face a series of unexpected developments in order to get to their happy ending. This story follows the conventions of the "wager tale" type that would often be used in the eighteenth century: a set of ideally matched lovers must solve a riddle in order to be able to unite (Robert, *Le conte de fées* 193–201). La Force's tales are also unusual for their implicit or explicit eroticism; in addition to the tale in this collection, "L'enchanteur," "Plus belle que fée" ("More Beautiful than a Fairy"), and "Persinette" also include erotic episodes. The pleasure that Princess Bleu takes in the gaze of her male admirer is truly unique in this genre and shows readers a nontraditional way of representing desire and love in fairy tales.

Further Reading

Dauphiné, Claude. *Charlotte-Rose de Caumont: Une romancière du XVIIe siècle.* P. Fanlac, 1980.

Duggan, Anne. "Women and Absolutism in French Opera and Fairy Tale." *The French Review,* no. 78, vol. 2, pp. 302–15.

La Force, Charlotte-Rose Caumont de. "Vert et Bleu." Robert, *Contes,* pp. 372–87.

Robert, Raymonde. "Charlotte-Rose Caumont de La Force." Robert, *Contes*, pp. 295–302.

———. *Le conte de fées littéraire en France de la fin du XVIIe siècle à la fin du XVIIIe siècle.* PU de Nancy, 1982.

———, editor. *Contes.* Champion, 2005. Bibliothèque des génies et des fées 2.

Seifert, Lewis. "Charlotte-Rose de Caumont de La Force (c. 1650–1724)." *The Teller's Tale: Lives of the Classic Fairy-Tale Writers*, edited by Sophie Raynard, State U of New York P, 2013, pp. 89–93.

Storer, Mary Elizabeth. *Un épisode littéraire à la fin du XVIIe siècle: La mode des contes de fées, 1685–1700.* Slatkine Reprints, 1972, pp. 109–28.

Vellenga, Carolyn. "Rapunzel's Desire: A Reading of Mlle de La Force." *Marvels and Tales*, vol. 6, no. 1, 1992, pp. 285–87.

Welch, Marcelle Maistre. "L'Éros féminin dans les contes de fées de Mlle de La Force." *Actes de Las Vegas*, edited by Marie-France Hilgar Papers on French Seventeenth-Century Literature, 1991, pp. 217–23. Biblio 17.

Green and Blue

There was once a queen who discovered that she was with child and so immediately summoned her sister, who went by the name of Sublime. Sublime was a fairy of profound and unerring knowledge, and her sister the queen wanted her present at the delivery to tell the child's future.

When the queen gave birth, the fairy took the little girl in her arms and studied her closely. She saw something wonderfully elevated in the baby's face, a nobility and a pride worthy of her royal blood, but she also saw that the girl would lead a life of sorrow if she loved any ordinary man. In a word, she realized that the girl would never be truly happy unless she was bound to one who deserved her love in every way but who was at the same time her absolute opposite, and that their love would have to surmount a great many obstacles before their union could ever come to pass.

Sublime was deeply saddened by her vision of the child's future and of all that stood in the way of a happy ending for her. Finding the girl's opposite would be hard enough, she thought, but harder still would be finding a perfect man, for Nature was no longer what she once had been: rarely indeed, no less rarely than today, did she produce a truly exceptional person.

The fairy wondered what she should do with the little princess; finally, determined to keep her out of men's clutches, she made a home for her in a cloud, along with her nurse and four other princesses of her age and of her blood. She fashioned the girl's home in the skies, far from the earth and its corruptions; with her attentive care, she hoped, she might one day make the princess a fine and accomplished young lady.

The princess had the loveliest eyes in the world, so blue and so bright that the intensity of her gaze turned the cloud the same color; thus it was that the fairy, when it came time to give her a name, dubbed her Princess Bleu.

Sublime endeavored to give the princess a soul as beautiful as her appearance was perfect; she was pleased to see the girl fulfill all her hopes. Bleu had the keenest natural intelligence on earth; the fairy enriched it with all the finest things there are to know, and apart from the dark arts nothing was alien to her.[1] Better still, the

---

1. The dark arts (or black magic, witchcraft) were a dangerous association for women during a time when witches were persecuted and killed. It is important to note the anxiety surrounding the super-

girl was as wise as she was learned. The fairy told her of the fate she must be sure to avoid, but the princess's pride naturally inclined her toward a happier lot; looking inside herself, she realized that she could never settle for any run-of-the-mill prince. Sublime was delighted to see her display such exacting tastes.

The fairy had not created Bleu's strange abode all alone. She was close friends with a great magician— more than friends, said some, who claimed that she and Tiphis (for such was his name) were in fact longtime lovers. This much alone was certain: that neither ever undertook a great project without the other's help, that they always openly shared their ideas, and that they lived together far from prying eyes.

Tiphis had a son by the name of Zélindor, the child of a queen he had once tenderly loved. That prince was so comely, so noble, and already so in love with the princess, whom he saw nearly every day, that Sublime sometimes thought Zélindor might be the glorious lover promised by destiny; but she soon abandoned that idea, for she could see no way in which he was the girl's opposite, and so long as Tiphis and herself consented to their union she could think of no obstacles they would have to overcome.

---

natural at this cultural moment in France. Bleu is associated with magic, but the author takes care to reinforce that the princess's powers are entirely grounded in wisdom.

But let us leave these good people of the air for a moment and come back to earth. Two years before Princess Bleu's birth, the universe was governed by a young monarch, his reign assured as much by his power as by his sweetness and charm; his beauty itself served to bring him new subjects. His name was Printemps.[2] The world lived happily under his reign, everything flourished under his agreeable rule, and the people of the earth loved each other to the point of adoration. But the fates soon took good Printemps away from them; his demise was the cause of deep mourning all over the world.

His wife the queen was pregnant at the time of his death. The philosophers, who in those days governed the calendar and the measurement of time, gave the beloved king's name to the most pleasant of all the seasons, which has preserved the name *printemps* ever since; and so, when the queen gave birth to a son who from his earliest age displayed all the charms of his father, it was clear that he had to be called Prince Vert.[3] Ever lively and cheerful, the child possessed beauty and charm beyond description; he was as deeply revered as the one who had given him life. In body and soul, he was the very image of his father, and worthy of him in every way.

---

2. In other words, Spring.
3. That is, Green.

His court was opulent and gallant, but none of the beauties vying to win his affections could boast that they had touched that proud heart, which Love nonetheless yearned to make its servant.

He had just won a difficult victory, vanquishing an aged king of legendary force, a tyrant who stripped all the world of its finery.[4] Now that that fight was behind him, the prince wanted only to celebrate, to fill his days with gallant festivities and continual distractions.

Word of his glory spread far and wide. He was not unknown to Tiphis and Sublime, who admired him no less than anyone else. Deep in his heart, Zélindor seethed with jealousy at Prince Vert's renown. Princess Bleu's emotions were stronger still: in her innermost thoughts, she could not help but be drawn to that charming prince, and to hope he might be the one promised her by the fates, even if it meant confronting a thousand ordeals.

She abandoned herself to these thoughts, knowing that she would never love an ordinary man, and however loving and worthy she found Zélindor, when she compared him to what she heard of Prince Vert, an ordinary man was all she could see in him.

The fairy Sublime read her thoughts and was pleased. Trusting the princess's sound good sense and uprightness of soul, she sometimes gave her leave to go down to

---

4. The aged prince would of course be Winter.

the mountains, and from there to the plains, where she could hunt with her four princesses. The fairy even created a beautiful fountain down in a valley, where the princess could bathe whenever she was weary and wanted to refresh herself.

Now and then Princess Bleu strolled a bit further on, into the towns, where she could enjoy the public entertainments and other amusements or curiosities. But Sublime wanted no one to see the princess's prodigious beauty, and so she made her invisible by means of a veil that concealed her from all human gazes: the Veil of Illusion, capable of hiding what is true and sometimes making the unreal seem real. Whenever the mood struck Bleu to visit the world of men, she had only to put it over her head, with the four corners held by the four princesses, and she could take on any appearance she liked—a beautiful edifice, a little hut, a grove of trees, an obelisk, as her whim dictated—and in that way she could go where she pleased in perfect safety.

One day she was out visiting a magnificent park when she heard the sounds of a hunt in progress. Quickly she unfurled her mysterious veil, willing herself to appear as a figure carved in girasol,[5] standing atop four sapphire pillars. Thus transformed, she watched the hunting party

---

5. Girasol: a stone in the quartz family, the color of milk, but, notably for this story, often with a light-blue tint.

go by several times, all of them crying out in amazement at the wondrous sight they were passing. Finally she spied a young horseman, in whom Nature had deployed every perfection she had to offer. The moment his eyes lit on that sculpture, he nimbly leapt to earth; for some time he studied the figure, which had all the traits and charms of the princess, and so resembled her that it seemed almost alive, then dropped to his knees in rapture and cried out, "O God! why must this wonder have been made by human hands?"

The princess gazed on that oddly agitated stranger; her eyes had never seen anything so charming. He was exceptionally tall, but his proportions were inexpressibly harmonious. His face was magnificent, with a glow from within, for the graces had endowed it with all their charms.

Bleu stood rapt in the contemplation of that perfect figure of a man, and the sight of him pierced her heart through and through. "Alas!" she thought. "Is this the man whose commonness is destined to cause me such misery? For outer beauty is nothing without the ornaments of a keen mind and a noble soul."

But her fears soon subsided, and she gave in to the certainty that he must be as fine inside as out.

As she stood absorbed in these thoughts, the prince studied the statue so closely that he came to forget everything around him. In a conspiratorial whisper, one of the young princesses asked Bleu to let them sing a song and make the stranger's confoundment complete.

Smiling, the good princess told her she thought that a fine idea, and so the four princesses sang out as follows:

> You see before you the only object that might
>   charm you[6]
> The only one you can love,
> Offering glorious chains to bind your heart,
> Precious chains forged by Love itself.
> Take heart, and remember that after many travails
> A glorious destiny may await you.

The prince was dumbstruck to hear such beautiful voices coming from the sapphire columns, united in a harmony that went straight to his soul and roused all the tender feelings inside it. He began to wonder if he was in his right mind; he asked himself if this was all some sort of enchantment, and if he would ever escape it. The words of the song were repeated too many times for him to miss even one of them, and so he let himself be swept away on a wave of happy hopes. "Tell me, then," he cried, "what must I do to deserve to burn with those fires, and to hope I will be repaid? What tasks would I not gladly take on? The labors of Hercules himself would not daunt me!"

---

6. Object (in French *objet*): The text is clearly referring to the princess herself.

A single voice answered him:

Seek out the object that today has pleased you.

The second voice continued:

Then it will be your turn to persuade and to please.

The third went on:

May love be your heart's sole concern.

And the fourth sang the conclusion:

For the price of love is love.

With that, Bleu and her princesses vanished, the veil hiding her from the stranger, who stood riveted to the spot, stunned, half in a daze. "Where have you gone?" he cried out, then found himself speechless. Finally he went on, "What has become of you, divine creature, whose image is even now so vividly imprinted on my heart? It must be a spell: some magic formula lies behind what I have just seen. Am I in love with a statue? Am I to be the Pygmalion of my time?"[7]

In vain did the poor prince struggle to summon his reason: it did not come to his rescue, and whatever he told himself of the chimera he was in love with, he loved

---

7. Pygmalion: the Greek mythical figure made famous in Ovid's *Metamorphoses*. Pygmalion is a sculptor who, though he is not interested in women, creates a sculpture of a woman so beautiful that he falls in love with his own creation. In an answer to his prayers, Aphrodite breathes life into the statue and the two become lovers. The story raises questions about the superiority of art over nature, the artist as godlike figure, and the nature of love in a world of disillusionment.

her still. That insistent, inescapable thought followed
and tormented him everywhere he went.

Bleu was no better off than he. She had resolved to disappear and to leave him only because she sensed that if
she stayed any longer she might be moved to reveal herself in her true form. Flight seemed her only protection,
the only remedy for a weakness that all her firm resolve
would could not shield her from.

Her heart was pounding as she made her way back to
her home in the clouds, and she well knew why. "So my
fate is sealed," she was thinking. "But is it a good fate, is
it bad? I'm in love with a stranger who could well be of
low birth, whose character might make me blush if I
knew of it. But no, if I can trust my heart's judgment, he
is in every way the perfect ideal of a man—how could he
possibly be unworthy of my love?"

Prince Zélindor sought out every opportunity to be
with her: the sight of him soon became intolerable, and
she faced him with a coldness that filled him with despair. She was by nature a kind and thoughtful person,
and the prince could not imagine what had brought about
such a change. She became contemplative, and therefore withdrawn; he began to fear that her mind might
be filled with thoughts of another man. He decided to
spy on her, and often followed the princess's footsteps
from afar.

One evening, after a long day of hunting, she headed for the magnificent fountain made specially for her by the fairy Sublime.

Clear waters rippled inside a shimmering opal, the last rays of the sun seeming to pierce them in search of their origin. But Bleu's eyes exerted a still more prodigious effect: her gaze seemed almost to set those waters aflame, and the land all around. She bathed, her beautiful body covered only by a transparent drape. Her princesses were with her as well, but for all their attempts to distract her, the handsome stranger alone filled her thoughts.

But what a joy, and what a surprise! For as she was frolicking with her friends she suddenly spied him leaning against a tree, gazing on her with eyes full of love.

He had to be Prince Vert, for what other man in the world could be made like him? He had come to that spot purely by chance, and was dumbstruck to discover the glorious original of the statue that still captivated his imagination, delighted that a girl such as this could exist in this world. He dared hope that she might not be unmoved by the love he had so quickly come to feel for her; perhaps, now that he had sought her everywhere and finally found her, the last lines that had been sung to him might even come true.

The princess caught sight of him as he was pondering these thoughts, marveling at the beauty before him. She had immersed herself in the water, but now she stood up without thinking, and so offered still more splendors to the amorous prince's gaze. The graces and proportions of that divine form sent him into such a transport of love that he could not help but tell her of his deep emotion. Bleu could not hide: she no longer had the Veil of Illusion to protect her, having left it on the ground with her clothes, and in truth she wasn't sorry, for she found a certain pleasure in the effect her beauty had produced. The prince's words were so elegant, and his sentiments seemed so noble and genuine, that the princess, heeding an instinct that can nearly always be trusted, felt sure he was the one whose birth the heavens had ordained for her happiness. She tried to find a cold, regal answer to give him, but she could summon up nothing more than mere modesty. Begging him to begone, she kept him there by her passionate manner; ordering him to speak no more of love, her eyes told him her heart was full of just that. Finally he agreed to do as she said, but as a price for his docility he gained her permission to come to this same place again the next day.

Once he was gone, the fair Bleu snatched up her clothes and lay down beside the water, waiting for her princesses to dress, but she had no time to daydream: Zélindor appeared, telling her he had witnessed all that had just transpired. She thought this odiously indiscreet, and she sharply rebuked him. "Ah!" he told her, "I have lost you."

And since a man in love has sharp eyes indeed, he guessed who his rival was: "It must be Prince Vert," he said. "There's no doubt about it."

"I almost suspected as much," the princess said to herself.

"You love him," he went on, "but my father's authority would be feeble indeed if I were powerless to prevent another from enjoying a possession Tiphis has already vouchsafed for me."[8]

He left her with these menacing words. The princess withdrew, resolving to confide in the fairy Sublime once she saw her lover again and assured herself that he was Prince Vert.

She suspected that Zélindor would be waiting for her at the meeting place the next day. She enlisted the aid of a pelican she was very fond of, a bird of keen intelligence. She placed the Veil of Illusion in its breast, through the opening by which pelicans feed their young;[9] the bird then brought it to the prince, enabling him to conceal himself from his rival's eyes.

---

8. If above, Prince Vert marvels at the self-objectification engineered by Princess Bleu, here, Zélindor's objectification of the princess as possession is entirely lacking in respect. The rhetorical tension between the two kinds of objectification further underscores the different natures of Zélindor and Vert.

9. A wide range of medieval and early modern illuminations and illustrations depict the pelican feeding its young through a hole in its breast.

He had come to wait by the fountain long before the appointed hour, as eager lovers do. The pelican presented him with the veil and taught him how to use it, whereupon Bleu set off for the fountain. Prince Vert ran to meet her as soon as he spied her in the distance, and he spoke to her with the deepest sincerity, passion, and tenderness. The princess sat down on the ground, and her lover adopted the form of a little flowered bramble bush. Kneeling next to Bleu, he confessed that he was Prince Vert. In turn, she revealed that she was the daughter of the queen of the Indies,[10] telling him of her life, and of the strange house she had been given to protect her from feelings she would regret if they were they not inspired by a prince of great merit, who had nonetheless to be in some way her opposite.

But these two were perfectly matched: they could see no sign of any opposition at all. How could they not have been destined to be together, since they already loved each other with such passion? Bleu told the prince she would speak to Sublime, for she was convinced that the fairy was wholeheartedly devoted to their interests. They then parted ways, after swearing eternal fidelity.

---

10. Refers to modern-day India; the point of this passage is simply that Bleu is of noble birth.

Zélindor was not far from the fountain, and when he spied the princess alone, with no sign of his rival, he suspected that something was afoot. But he did not want to confront her, and so he walked away—just a few steps behind Prince Vert, as it happened. Thinking no harm could come of it, the young prince took off the veil, and thus revealed himself undisguised. No words could express Zélindor's fury; now he knew that his rival and his mistress were in collusion. Spurred on by the force of his jealousy, he went to find Tiphis and poured out his sorrows. Tiphis listened attentively, as any loving father would, but he shared his grief in the manner of a man whose power knows no bounds, which was another thing entirely.

He went straight off to complain to the fairy Sublime, who had just been told of all this by Princess Bleu; he did not find her disposed to share his sentiments. Their conversation soon grew so heated that they parted ways in anger. The fairy had laughed out loud when Tiphis spoke of giving Bleu to Zélindor, answering that his son was nowhere near worthy of one so perfect as Bleu.

Their friendship at an end, Tiphis and Sublime returned to their homes; meanwhile, Princess Bleu sent her faithful pelican back to Prince Vert to inform him of all that had happened and to name a place where they might meet: a wood full of musk rose trees, all ringed with jasmines. Such a pleasant place seemed made for the happiness of those perfect lovers. Separately, they hurried toward the wood. Spying each other at the opposite ends of a prodigiously long, wide pathway, they both broke into a gentle run, but all at once they felt something hobbling their gait: nets had sprung up from the ground, holding them fast. They were still far apart; they could see each other clearly, but they could not speak. (In love, seeing is enough if nothing more can be had.) The suffering lovers tried a hundred times to free themselves, but in vain, and their struggles bore eloquent witness to their grief.

The four princesses realized that they had been snared in the same way, powerless to do anything but weep with Bleu over this sad turn of events.

Finally darkness fell. It was unheard of for someone of Bleu's rank to spend the night in this way; having no other choice, she resigned herself, but did so not without tears.

The next day dawned, and the rising sun revealed a sumptuously decorated garden swing, with a wide, magnificently crafted seat hanging from gold and blue silk ropes clasped by four winged children, who held the swing in place. Prince Zélindor alighted from the swing, cut lovely Bleu free, and invited her to come and sit beside him. She tried to resist, but he forcibly sat her down on the seat, then took his place beside her.

What a sorrow for her, forced to abandon the man she loved and follow the one she loathed! And what a sight for Prince Vert, his rival carrying off his beloved before his eyes!

For as long as she'd lived, Bleu had never been without her four princesses; she bade them a loving farewell, and the poor women pierced the air with their mournful cries.

The swing lifted off the ground, then paused close by the wretched Prince Vert. As a further insult to the grieving prince, Zélindor sang these words:

> Nothing can rival the depth of my love,
> Nothing can rival my joy;
> O, my blissful heart, cry out in delight
> For my beloved is now mine alone.

The princess keenly felt the blow Zélindor was dealing Prince Vert; drawing on the fires of her love, she tearfully told him:

> Ever faithful will I be,
> Never shall my flame be snuffed out,
> Not by your rival, not by death itself.
> Let us love each other tenderly, you and I,
> And let us endure our cruel fate;
> When two hearts are joined in a perfect love,
> The day of their happiness will surely come.

She wept as she sang. Operas were only beginning to be written in that age, and that technique is still used to this day.[11]

Taken aback by such a forceful expression of love, Zélindor had his swing lift off again, and it did not stop until it reached Tiphis's superb palace. The gardens were particularly marvelous: the gardens of Versailles were created on that very model.[12]

Every day new pleasures were lavished on the princess, and for a woman of flighty and flirtatious spirit those pleasantly varied days would have seemed woven of silk and gold, but the faithful princess found only bitterness in them, and every day seemed to last a century, with Zélindor always near and Prince Vert so far away.

Tiphis himself took pains to sway the princess in favor of his son and convince her that he was the true lover promised her by the fates. He told her she would find no greater opposition than that between their two hearts, for Zélindor's burned for her, and hers was as cold as ice toward him. "Ah! enough," answered the princess. "What pitiful reasoning! Heaven promised me happiness

---

11. Scholars such as Anne Duggan have explored the relationship between opera and the development of the literary *conte* in the seventeenth century.

12. La Force is creating a link here between Tiphis's magical gardens and the palatial grounds of Louis XIV: by suggesting that the literary garden inspired the Sun King himself, the text establishes a genealogy and a sense of superiority, at the same time aligning Tiphis's creation with the magnificence of Versailles by association.

through some sort of opposition, but that cannot mean an opposition in the heart. I can never be happy if I do not love as much as I am loved."[13]

Such was the sad life she lived in that splendid palace. Meanwhile, the fairy Sublime, surprised not to see her come home, sent the pelican out to look for her. So diligently did the faithful pelican search that just one day after Bleu's disappearance he found the pleasant wood where the prince and the four princesses were still trapped. He severed their bonds with his beak and his talons. Prince Vert embraced him a thousand times in gratitude, and the bird made ready to convey the princesses back to the fairy Sublime. The prince said many beautiful things to them, and they to him, but they had no choice but to part.

And so Prince Vert left the little wood, finding before him only a vast plain, sterile and treeless. He set off walking, but the sun was high in the sky, and the heat soon became more than he could bear, particularly after three days with nothing to eat. He sensed he was close to breathing his last. He tried to return to the little wood in search of relief, but he could find no way in, and his feet

---

13. This is a strong declaration in an age when women rarely married for love and, indeed, openly expressed disillusionment in the institution of marriage. Even texts describing happy matches tend to be cautious about the potential disappointments, pitfalls, and risks of love. Readers see here a rare moment of optimism voiced by a woman intent on finding love for herself.

led him willy-nilly back to that fearsome open expanse, so dry and so hostile.

Terrible indeed was his torment. He was in desperate need of some tender thought to quell his violent ideas, for many times he was tempted to run himself through with his sword. In that dire state he lifted his eyes toward the burning sun and found that darkness seemed to have fallen, even though the air was as hot as ever. He stood wondering what to make of this when all of a sudden he spied a movement in the sky: it was a multitude of birds, of all species and all colors, from the phoenix to the wren. At the head of that legion flew his bearer of good news: his beloved pelican, who alighted beside the prince as some of his fellow birds landed on the ground and the others hovered in the air, all of them soon pressing together to create a palace, one of a sort never before seen in this world.

Dumb with astonishment, the prince entered through a magnificent portico. The rooms glowed with a thousand colors. The floors were the shells of those birds' eggs, and the ceilings the stuff from which they make their marvelous nests.

By that magical abode, the fairy Sublime had once again revealed her power over the air, which she had made the lifelong home of the cherished princess. The pelican served Prince Vert devotedly, and he was able to enjoy all the most delicious foods on earth.

He could not stop thinking of Princess Bleu. He had just made up his mind to ask the pelican to go looking for her when a woman of cheerful countenance arrived at the palace with the four princesses in tow. Guessing that she must be the fairy Sublime, he threw himself at her feet. She gave him a thousand tender greetings, and she beamed with joy as she spoke: "I thought I would never learn how to put an end to the sufferings you and Princess Bleu have endured, for Tiphis is every bit as skilled and learned as I. But finally, after long pondering your plight, I realized that his spell would be broken the moment I found in what way you and your beloved are opposites. Then I would have only to follow my pelican to find the princess and take her back.

"I racked my brains in search of the opposition, but nothing came to mind. I will freely admit to my foolishness: I never did find it. For six months I lived in a state of continual worry, separated from the girl I so love, who deserves all the affection I can give her.

"One day I was mournfully walking in the country, and idly I stopped to admire the noble economy of the ants. I saw before me one of their little republics absorbed in its daily labors, and I looked on with pleasure. But just then I realized that the ants were spelling out letters, that those tiny bodies joined together distinctly formed these words:

It is in the names of the lovers

That the end of their sorrows can be found.

"I clapped my hands in astonishment and let out a great burst of laughter: 'How stupid I am!' I cried. 'O human prudence, how blind you are! The simplest sometimes know better than the wise.'" A hundred times I marveled that so obvious a thing could have so long eluded me: the ordinary people of this world have always thought blue and green two entirely incompatible colors![14] But my hope is that I will soon bring them together forever, through the union of two people who bear their names.

"And so here I am," the fairy concluded. "Now, I beg you, let us hurry off to Tiphis's palace without further delay, for there we will find the princess."

"Will she still be faithful?" the prince asked.

"I give you my word," answered Sublime.

"Then let us be off," he said. The wise pelican took wing at once, followed by the entire flying edifice, and they made a quick journey that promised to end in nothing but pleasure.

That palace stopped close by Tiphis's, whose doors opened all on their own. The fairy Sublime entered unhindered, holding Prince Vert by the hand, the four princesses following behind.

---

14. Blue and green are clashing colors on a traditional color wheel.

Stunned to see them before him, Tiphis could not think what to say or do. Princess Bleu, who had been sitting lost in thought by a fountain named Lancelade, heard the to-do and turned her head.[15] Catching sight of those she loved most in the world, she leapt up and ran to them in a transport of joy. "And so I see you again," cried the prince, kneeling at her feet, "and you see me, as faithful as I promised."

The fairy had no wish to waste time in frivolous speeches, or in amusement at Zélindor's despair, and so she hurried them into their flying palace, which carried them to the queen of the Indies, the mother of Princess Bleu.

What joy for her! What delight for those faithful lovers! The festivities went on and on, and everything was elegant and superb.

On their wedding day, the fairy Sublime gave them clothes of a most extraordinary kind: those enchanted garments were woven from delicate grasses, studded with blue hyacinths, and their mantles were similarly lined with a velvety moss of the freshest green.

They were so fine a sight in that simple, beautiful raiment, so closely aligned with their names, that no one could look away. Heaven received a thousand prayers for

---

15. "Lancelade" is quite likely a reference to one of the fountains in the gardens of Versailles, today called the Bosquet de l'Encelade.

their prosperity, which proved long and unshakable, for their love never faded. Only the union of two hearts can create real happiness in this life.

> A trifle can separate two lovers,
> A confusion drive them apart,
> And when it does, what tender moments
> A loving heart denies itself!

One of the great princes of Europe once heard this tale, and he found it so pleasant, and Prince Vert so appealing, that he bore his name with great success.[16]

---

16. In the Champion edition, Raymonde Robert notes that this could be a reference to Louis XIV himself (La Force, "Vert et Bleu" 387n1). By suggesting that Louis adopted this name for himself, La Force would be associating the *conte* with the king, a move that would elevate the story's renown. Lewis C. Seifert and Domna C. Stanton add the possibility of Henri IV (1553–1610), who was often called Vert Galant because of his flirtatious tendencies (La Force, "Green and Blue" 229n375).

Marie-Jeanne L'héritier de Villandon

(1664–1734)

Unlike many of the other *conteuses* of her time, Marie-Jeanne L'héritier de Villandon lived a life free from scandals. Born in Paris, she was related to Charles Perrault through her mother, Françoise Le Clerc, who was either the sister or the niece of Perrault's mother. L'héritier's father, who served as historiographer to Louis XIV, insisted on giving his daughter a good education, and her erudition is made clear by her 1732 translation of Ovid's *Heroides*. A frequent contributor to the *Mercure galant*, L'héritier also won a prize from the Académie des Palinots of Caen and twice won competitions by the Académie des Lanternistes of Toulouse. She was admitted to the Toulouse Academy in 1696.

Though the claim has not been substantiated, many believe that L'héritier held a literary salon that was attended by Marie-Catherine d'Aulnoy, Catherine Bernard, and Henriette-Julie de Castelnau, comtesse de Murat. According to some sources, she even inherited Madeleine de Scudéry's salon after the latter's death (*Éloge*). Whether or not these claims are true, it is clear that L'héritier was one of the strongest defenders of women's writing in her time. Her reputation for moral rectitude earned recognition during her life and at the time of her death in 1734, when the *Journal des sçavans* published an extensive and laudatory obituary. Yet while L'héritier is clear in her defense of education and protofeminist ideals, she tries to assimilate feminist arguments with classically held views about women, insisting on the importance of virtue (a combination of submission, chastity, and education). L'héritier consciously participates in the formation of the literary fairy tale genre, whose history and aesthetic she addresses in her *Lettre à Madame de D.G.**** (1695; *Letter to Madame de D.G.****). In her *Œuvres meslées* (*Various Works*), L'héritier also makes reference to the *contes* of Murat, though they would not be published for three more years. Thus, L'héritier's writings make clear that she was on good personal terms with other participants in the genre and that they told their stories orally before committing them to print versions.

L'héritier's *contes* are stylistically closer to those of d'Aulnoy and Murat than to those of Bernard, Charlotte-Rose Caumont de La Force, or Perrault. Filled with digressions and winding plot twists, her *contes* more closely resemble novellas than they do fairy tales. This is evident in both stories included in this volume. In her tales, L'héritier upholds the merits of chastity. The heroine Finette in "L'adroite princesse" ("The Quick-Witted Princess") engages in numerous wild adventures and exploits, but they are all in the name of resisting the prince's advances and protecting her sisters' reputations (and, by association, her own). Today's readers will appreciate the strong female lead; they may also question how far it is appropriate to go in order to exact revenge and restore one's honor.

The plot of "Les enchantements de l'éloquence" ("The Wonders of Eloquence") closely follows that of Perrault's "Les fées" ("The Fairies"): in fact, L'héritier's version contains numerous allusions to her uncle's version, and the two were probably written as a friendly competition. Perrault's version is much shorter and simpler: its entire intrigue is focused on the fountain scene. L'héritier adds depth to the characters and insists on the merits of reading and eloquence for women. The heroine, Blanche, looks to antiquity for examples of virtuous

and obedient women in order to defend her own love of reading and to help her bear the burdens of physical labor. It is her
eloquence and education that gain her the favors of the fairies.
Perrault's tale, on the other hand, reduces the two girls to their
essential natures—beauty and goodness on the one hand, ugliness and spitefulness on the other.

Further Reading

Delbrun, R. P. Pierre. *Le grand apparat français, avec le latin
   recueilli de Ciceron, et des principaux auteurs de la langue latine.*
   9th ed., Richard Lallemant et Eustache Viret, 1679.

Duby, George. *The Knight, the Lady, and the Priest: The Making of
   Modern Marriage in Medieval France.* Translated by Barbara
   Bray, U of Chicago P, 1984.

"Éloge de Mademoiselle l'Héritier." *Journal des sçavans*, vol. 3,
   Sept.-Dec. 1734, pp. 832–36.

Lebas, Catherine, and Annie Jacques. *La coiffure en France du
   Moyen Âge à nos jours.* Delmas, 1979.

Seifert, Lewis. *Fairy Tales, Sexuality, and Gender in France,
   1690–1715: Nostalgic Utopias.* Cambridge UP, 1996. Cambridge
   Studies in French 55.

———. "Marie-Jeanne L'Héritier de Villandon (1664–1734)." *The
   Teller's Tale: Lives of the Classic Fairy-Tale Writers*, edited by
   Sophie Raynard, State U of New York P, 2013, pp. 75–80.

———. "The Rhetoric of *Invraisemblance*: Lhéritier's 'Les
   Enchantements de l'éloquence.'" *Cahiers du dix-septième*,
   vol. 3, no. 1, 1989, pp. 121–39.

Seifert, Lewis C., and Domna C. Stanton. Introduction.
   *Enchanted Eloquence: Fairy Tales by Seventeenth-Century French
   Women Writers*, edited and translated by Seifert and Stanton,
   Center for Reformation and Renaissance Studies, Iter, 2010,
   pp. 1–45. The Other Voice in Early Modern Europe: The
   Toronto Series 9.

Storer, Mary Elizabeth. *Un épisode littéraire à la fin du XVIIᵉ siècle:
   La mode des contes de fées, 1685–1700.* Slatkine Reprints, 1972,
   pp. 42–60.

The Quick-Witted Princess;
or, Finette's Adventures

To Madame la Comtesse de Murat[1]

You write the most wonderful stories in verse, and your verse is as musical as it is natural. I long to tell you a story of my own, charming countess, but I do not know what you might think of it. I find myself in the mood of the Bourgeois Gentilhomme today:[2] I would like to tell this story neither in verse nor in prose, without big words, without eloquence, without rhyme. A naive style suits me best. In short, my story will be simply told, and told as people speak. I mean to express only a lesson.

---

1. Henriette-Julie de Castelnau, comtesse de Murat, another leading figure of the French fairy tale vogue and author of "The Pleasant Punishment" and "Anguillette" in this volume.

2. In Molière's 1670 comedy *Le bourgeois gentilhomme*, Monsieur Jourdain, an obtuse but ambitious member of the bourgeoisie, seeks a proper education to make him a gentleman (*gentilhomme*). When he asks his teacher how to write a beautiful love letter, the teacher asks him if he would like the letter to be in prose or in verse, and he answers that he wants neither one (failing to understand that those are the only two possibilities).

There are several in my little story, and in that way it might please you. It turns around two proverbs rather than one, for that is the fashion, and you are fond of that fashion, so I follow it gladly. Here you will see how our foremothers conveyed the message that we go astray in a thousand ways when we delight in doing nothing; or, to put it as they did, that *idleness is the mother of all vice.*[3] And no doubt you will appreciate their demonstration that we must forever be on our guard: in other words, as you will have understood, that *wariness is the mother of safety.*

> No, love does not conquer
> Only hearts with no occupation.
> You who fear that a wily victor
> Will make a fool of your reason,
> Young lovelies, if you want to protect your hearts,
> Then you must occupy your minds.
> But if, for all your efforts, you are fated to love,
> Then at least take care not to be charmed
> Before you truly know
> The one your heart wants as its master.
> Avoid the flattersome popinjays
> Who always appear wherever ladies gather,
> And, not knowing what to say to a beautiful woman,

---

3. Idleness in a woman was seen as a dangerous threat to her chastity.

Heave heavy sighs though they feel no love.[4]

You must sound the depths of their minds,

For they declaim a thousand empty words

    to every Iris.

Be wary, then, of those quick workers

Who claim to burn with love from the very

    first sight

And swear their flame is burning bright.

Pay no mind to their hollow promises:

It takes time to subjugate a soul.

Do not let your good will

Strip you too soon of your austere reserve,

For your sensible caution alone

Will protect your tranquility and your safety.

But what have I done, Madame—I have lapsed into verse! I have not kept to the tastes of Monsieur Jourdain at all: I have rhymed like Quinault![5] I now hasten to return to the simple manner, lest I become a target for the contempt so many feel toward that agreeable moralist, and lest I be accused of copying and stealing from him, as so many merciless writers do every day.

---

4. These lines are reminiscent of Perrault's moral at the end of "Le petit chaperon rouge" ("Little Red Riding Hood"), which calls amorous men such as these the most dangerous wolves of all (212).

5. Philippe Quinault, a French poet and librettist, is known for his long period of collaboration with the composer Jean-Baptiste Lully.

In the days of the first crusades, the monarch of I know not what kingdom of Europe resolved to set off for Palestine to battle the Infidels.[6] Before he embarked on that journey, he put his kingdom's affairs in order and entrusted the regency to his ablest minister; on that score his mind was at rest. What worried him more was the well-being of his family. He had lost his wife the queen not long before; she left him no sons, but he was the father of three young princesses of marriageable age. My chronicle does not tell me their true names; I know only that—since the simple people of that happy time freely gave nicknames to eminent personages, according to their qualities or their failings—the eldest princess was called *Nonchalante* (which in those days signified what today we mean by "lazy"), the second *Babillarde*, and the third *Finette*, and each of those names truly expressed the character of each sister.

No one had ever seen a living being as indolent as Nonchalante. She was never awake before one hour past noon. Straight out of bed, she had to be dragged off to church, with her hair uncombed, her dress not pinned

---

6. The First Crusade took place from approximately 1096 to 1099. The route began in France. The "Infidels" are the Muslim inhabitants of the lands that the Crusaders set out to reclaim for Christian Europe. The Crusades were long over by the time these stories were written; to a modern ear, this reference to the hoary cliché of "battling the Infidels" sounds distinctly ironic, particularly given these tales' supreme indifference to questions of religion. It's difficult to know whether that's the spirit in which L'héritier intends it.

up, no belt, and often two unmatched slippers. At some point later in the day that mistake would be corrected, but the princess could not be convinced to wear anything other than slippers: she found wearing shoes an unbearable fatigue. After her dinner, she sat down to make up her face, and did not rise again until evening. She then had her supper and gambled until midnight, when it took almost as long to undress her as it had to dress her. Never did she crawl into bed until well after sunup. Babillarde's life was of a very different sort. She was not one for resting, and spent little time on her appearance; but she had such an enormous compulsion to talk that her mouth never closed from the moment she woke up until she was asleep again. She knew all the gossip, and everything that went on—unhappy marriages, love affairs, and flirtations—among not only the entire court but even the most obscure commoners. In her head she had a catalogue of all the wives who raided the household budget to bedeck themselves in fine clothes, and she knew the exact wages of Countess X's maid and Marquis Y's butler. She learned all this by way of her nurse and her seamstress, whose conversation she preferred to any ambassador's; she then relentlessly repeated those edifying tales into the ears of anyone who would listen, from her father the king to his footmen, because as long as she was talking, it mattered not to whom. And the princess's unquellable urge to talk had another consequence: despite her high rank, her overly familiar manner emboldened all the love-hungry young men of the court to whisper sweet nothings in her ear. She listened to their honeyed words without hesitation, simply for the pleasure of answering, because, no matter what, she had to be listening or chattering from morning to night. No more than Nonchalante did Babillarde ever spend a single moment in thought, meditation, or reading. Nor did either one trouble herself with any sort of domestic chores or the pleasures of the needle and the spindle. In short, those two eternally unproductive sisters never exercised their minds or their hands.

The youngest princess was nothing like her sisters. Her mind and body were never idle; she was bursting with vitality, and she strove to make the best use of it. She was an exceptional dancer, singer, and musician, and had a great talent for all the little handcrafts that ordinarily amuse those of her sex. She brought order and respect for rules to the king's household, and put an end to thievery among the servants—for in those days servants did indeed dare to steal from kings.

Her gifts did not end there. She was perceptive and fast-thinking, and could find a way out of any difficulty as soon as she began looking for one. Thanks to her sharp eye, that young princess had once discovered a trap that a treacherous ambassador had laid for her father the king in a treaty he was on the point of signing. To punish the perfidy of that ambassador and his master, the king changed the treaty's wording in terms suggested by his daughter, and so he deceived the deceiver himself. The young princess then discovered another underhanded trick that a minister was trying to play, and with her aid and advice the king turned the perpetrator's ill intentions against him. The princess showed her shrewdness and intelligence on many other occasions, so often that the people took to calling her Finette.[7] The king loved her far more than his other daughters, and had such faith in her that he would have gone off to the crusades without a care had she been his only child; but for all his confidence in Finette he could not trust her sisters to behave themselves in his absence. And so, in order to be as sure of his family's conduct as he believed he could be of his subjects' allegiance, he took the measures I shall now recount.

You who so well know the ways of old, charming countess, I am certain you have heard tell a hundred times of the marvelous power of fairies. The king was a close friend of such a woman; he went to see her and told her of his worries. "I do not mean to say," he told her, "that my two eldest have ever done anything they shouldn't, but they are so mindless and heedless, and live such idle lives, that I fear they may fall into some foolish misadventure

---

7. In French, to be *fin* (or, in the feminine, *fine*) is to be clever, incisive, subtle, and so on.

simply for the sake of amusement. Of Finette's virtue I have no doubt, but I will treat her like the others, so that everything will be equal. And so, wise Fairy, I would like you to make me three glass distaffs,[8] each fashioned in such a way as to break the moment its owner does anything that brings shame on herself."

This was a particularly deft fairy, and so she gave the king three enchanted distaffs crafted with all necessary care and attention—but he was not satisfied with that single precaution. He took the princesses to a tall tower, built in a very out-of-the-way place. The king told his daughters they would live in this tower for as long as he was away, forbidding them to receive visitors of any kind. He sent away all their servants, male and female alike; then, once he had given his daughters the enchanted distaffs and explained their powers, he embraced the three princesses and locked the tower door behind him, taking the key. And with that he set off on his journey.

You may be thinking, Madame, that the princesses were in danger of starving, but no. A pulley had been attached to one of the tower's windows, with a rope and a basket that the princesses lowered to the ground every day for the delivery of their provisions; when they drew it

---

8. A distaff holds raw wool or linen so that it may be spun. Since spinning is traditionally women's work (see also the references to "needle" and "spindle" elsewhere in this tale), the distaff often serves as an emblem of femininity, as in the English expression "the distaff side."

up again they always took care to pull the rope into the room.

Nonchalante and Babillarde despaired of the life they lived in that lonely place; they were bored beyond all telling, but they had no choice but to endure it, for their distaffs were so delicately fashioned that they feared the slightest transgression would shatter them.

But Finette was not bored at all. She found all the amusement she needed in her spindle, her needle, and her musical instruments. And there was more, for the minister-regent had suggested that letters be regularly left in the princesses' basket, to keep them informed of all the latest happenings both inside and outside the kingdom; the king granted his permission, and the minister, wanting to ensure the princesses' favor, never failed to diligently perform that service. Finette always read the news with great interest and pleasure. Her two sisters never deigned to do the same, claiming that they were too miserable to amuse themselves with so little; it would take at the very least a deck of cards to keep them entertained. And so they sadly spent their days, bemoaning their fate, and I have no doubt that they often said, *It is better to be born happy than to be born the child of a king.*

They often stood at the tower windows so they could at least watch the goings-on in the countryside. One day, as Finette was busy in her room with a pretty piece of needlework, her sisters looked down from the window and saw a woman in tattered rags, piteously bewailing her poverty. With joined hands she begged them to let her into their chateau, telling them she was a poor stranger who knew a thousand sorts of things, and offering to serve them with the most scrupulous fidelity. At first the princesses remembered their father's order that no one be allowed into the tower; but Nonchalante was so tired of looking after herself, and Babillarde so bored with only her sister to talk to, that the yearning for a hairdresser and a conversation partner compelled them to let the poor stranger in.

"Do you really think the king's orders include people like this poor woman?" said Babillarde to her sister. "I'm quite sure we have nothing to fear from her."

"Do as you please, sister," answered Nonchalante. Babillarde, who was waiting only for her sister's consent, immediately lowered the basket. The beggar-woman climbed in, and the princesses pulled her up to the window.

Once the woman was standing before them, they were appalled by the wretched state of her dress. They wanted to give her new clothes, but she told them that could wait until the morrow; for the moment, she would see about serving them. Finette returned from her room just as the woman was finishing that sentence, and she was greatly surprised to see this stranger with her sisters. They told her why they had allowed her in; Finette hid her displeasure at their imprudence, for she could see all too well that there was no way to undo what was done.

Meanwhile the princesses' new servant walked all through the chateau, on the pretext of serving them but in truth for the purpose of observing its layout. For, Madame, perhaps you suspect this already, that supposed beggar-woman was in fact as great a menace in their chateau as Count Ory in the convent he entered disguised as a fearful abbess.[9]

I will keep you in suspense no longer: I will tell you at once that this ragged mendicant was in fact the oldest son of a powerful king, a neighbor of the princesses' father. One of the wiliest minds of his day, the young prince had his father entirely under his thumb, which required no great finesse, for the king was so mild and tolerant that he had been given the nickname *Moult-Bénin*.[10] As for the young prince, who acted only by artifice and deception, the people had come to call him *Riche-en-Cautèle*, and *Riche-Cautèle* for short.[11]

He had a younger brother, as fine and good as his elder was wicked; nonetheless, despite the difference in their natures, those two enjoyed a friendship so strong

---

9. The legend of the comte d'Ory is an old popular French tale. In it, the count and fourteen of his knights disguise themselves as nuns in order to enter a convent and sleep with the nuns and abbess. It inspired *Le comte Ory*, an opera by Gioachino Rossini.

10. Literally, "very gentle" or "very indulgent."

11. To be "riche en cautèle" would be to be full of cunning.

that it was the amazement of all. Apart from the virtue of the younger son's soul, the beauty of his face and the elegance of his figure were so remarkable that they had earned him the name *Bel-à-Voir.*[12] It was Prince Riche-Cautèle who had pushed his father's ambassador into the act of bad faith that Finette's skill had so adroitly turned against them. Riche-Cautèle had never been fond of the princesses' father, but when his misdeed was punished he conceived a genuine loathing for him; thus, on learning of the king's precautions concerning his daughters, he took a cruel pleasure in the thought of outwitting him. Having invented a pretext, Riche-Cautèle got his father's permission to set off on a voyage, then took the steps you have just seen to gain entrance into the tower.

Studying the chateau, the prince realized that the princesses could easily make themselves heard by anyone walking past, and he concluded that he would have to go on wearing his disguise until nightfall lest they cry out for help and have him punished for his brazen enterprise. All day long, then, he maintained his disguise as a beggar-woman; but once evening had come and the three sisters had supped, Riche-Cautèle threw off his rags; beneath them he wore a riding suit studded with gemstones and gold. Shocked, the poor princesses fled in panic. The fleet-footed Finette and Babillarde were the

---

12. "Beautiful to see."

first to reach their rooms; Nonchalante, for whom simply walking was an exertion, quickly found the prince
blocking her way.

He threw himself at her feet and announced who he
was, assuring her that he had heard so much of her beauty,
and had so often seen it for himself in her portraits,[13] that in
the end he could not do otherwise than to leave the luxury of his father's court to offer her his vows and his
honor. Nonchalante was too taken aback to answer the
kneeling prince, and so he went on, pouring out a thousand sweet words and protesting his love in a thousand
ways, finally begging her to take him as her own then
and there. She was by nature too lazy to argue, and so she
feebly told Riche-Cautèle that she found him sincere and
accepted his offer. And so, without further ado, they were
wed;[14] but that was the end of her distaff, which immediately shattered.

Meanwhile, Babillarde and Finette were trembling in
terror, locked in their bedrooms. Their rooms were not

---

13. Portrait halls, often filled with magical portraits with the powers
to move or talk, are common features of these fairy tales. In real life,
portraits were often copied and circulated to potential suitors and
were thus an important economic and social currency. For another example in this volume, see Murat's "Pleasant Punishment."

14. Seventeenth-century readers would have understood the sexual
innuendo being communicated here: during the French Middle Ages,
when the story is set, verbally consensual and sexually consummated
marriages were considered to be valid and binding, though the conventions and regulations defining marriage were disputed and contested repeatedly throughout the medieval period (see Duby).

close together, and since neither princess knew what had become of her sisters, they both spent the night wide awake. The next day, the wicked prince led Nonchalante into a little room at the far end of the garden, where the princess told Riche-Cautèle her sisters would be terribly worried about her, but she did not dare go to them, thinking they might scold her for this abrupt marriage. Assuring her that he would find a way to gain their approval, the prince took his leave, locking Nonchalante in the room without her realizing it. He then began a painstaking search for the princesses. Hours went by, and still he could not find where they were hiding. But Babillarde could not bear to keep silent; she sat in her room complaining out loud to herself. Hearing the sound of her voice, the prince crept to her door, bent down, and spied her through the keyhole.

Through the door, Riche-Cautèle told her what he had told her sister: that he had only sought entrance to the tower so that he could offer her his heart and his hand. He lavishly extolled her beauty and her mind, and Babillarde, who was entirely convinced of her own exceptional merit, was foolish enough to believe him. She answered with a torrent of more or less sensible words. She could never have managed to acquit herself as well as she did were it not for her all-consuming urge to speak, because she was utterly exhausted, not to mention that she'd had no food all day, since there was nothing decent to eat in her room. Unwilling to work, her mind occupied solely with talking endlessly, the princess never thought beyond the moment; when she needed something, she always turned to Finette, and that good-hearted princess, who was as hardworking and provident as her sisters were not, always had in her room a vast store of marzipans, fruit jellies, and preserves, both liquid and dry, made by her own hands. Lacking that advantage, pressed by hunger and by the prince's effusions, Babillarde ended up opening her door to that seducer, and once it was open he kept up his act, for he had carefully practiced his part.

They left the room together and went off to the chateau's kitchens, where they found all manner of refreshments, so generously provided by the basket. At first, Babillarde was still anxious about the fate of her sisters, but soon she convinced herself—on what grounds I know not—that they had probably both locked themselves into Finette's room, where they would have everything they might need. Riche-Cautèle eagerly confirmed that idea, and told her they would go and find the princesses once evening came. But to that she did not agree; she answered that they would have to go looking for them as soon as they'd had something to eat.

Finally the prince and the princess ate together in excellent humor, and when they were done, Riche-Cautèle asked her to show him the chateau's fine main rooms; he held out his hand for the princess to lead him, and when they were there he once again began to vigorously declare his love, vaunting the advantages she would find if she married him. As with Nonchalante, he told her that she must accept his vow right there on the spot, because if she talked to her sisters before she had taken him as her husband they would surely protest: he was by far the most powerful prince in all the surrounding kingdoms, and would thus seem a more suitable match for the eldest daughter than for her. That princess would never consent to their union, a union that he yearned for with all imaginable ardor. In the end, after all manner of empty words from the prince, Babillarde proved as foolish as her sister; she took the prince as her mate, and remembered the enchantment of her glass distaff only after it had broken into a hundred pieces.

Toward evening, Babillarde retired to her room with the prince, and the first thing she saw was her shattered distaff. She was greatly shaken by that sight, and the prince asked what was troubling her. Too fixated on talking to keep a secret, she carelessly revealed the mystery of the distaffs to Riche-Cautèle, who took an ignoble pleasure in the knowledge that they would give the princesses' father indisputable proof of his daughters' misconduct.

Babillarde had no wish to go looking for her sisters; rightly, she feared they would disapprove of what she had done. The prince offered to find them himself, and told her he would not fail to sway them to her side. Reassured, exhausted after a sleepless night, the princess soon drifted off, and as she slept Riche-Cautèle locked her in, just as he had done with Nonchalante.

Beautiful Countess, was this Riche-Cautèle not a despicable scoundrel, and were those two princesses not terribly incautious and gullible? I am very unhappy with them all, and I am sure you are too, but have no fear: they will get exactly what they deserve. Only brave, wise Finette will triumph.

Once the perfidious prince had imprisoned Babillarde, he set about searching every other room in the chateau, finding them all unlocked but one, which was barred from within; this, he concluded, had to be Finette's chosen hiding place. Having composed one all-purpose speech in his head, he stood outside Finette's door and spoke the same words as he had to her sisters; but the princess, not so easily taken in, simply listened in silence. Finally, realizing that he knew she was there, she told him that if his feelings for her were indeed as deep and sincere as he claimed, he would not mind going down to the garden and closing the gate behind him; then she would speak to him all he liked from her window above.

But Riche-Cautèle would not agree, and since Finette was still stubbornly refusing to let him into her room, the wicked prince stormed off to find a log with which to bash down the door. This was soon done, and inside he found Finette armed with a large hammer that happened to have been left in a cabinet close by her room. Her face was red with emotion, and despite the anger in her eyes, Riche-Cautèle found her enchantingly beautiful. He tried to kneel at her feet, but she backed away, sternly warning him, "Prince, if you come near me I will split your head open."

"Really, my beautiful Princess," Riche-Cautèle cajoled her in tender tones, "is this how a man's love for you is repaid, with such fearsome hatred?" He told her again, now from across the room, of the passion he had come to feel on hearing of her beauty and her exceptional mind. He added that he had only donned this disguise so that he could come and respectfully offer her his heart and his hand, and that she should blame his boldness in beating down the door on the entirely understandable force of his emotion. Just as he had her sisters, he tried to convince her that she would do well to take him as her husband at once. He told her he had no idea where her sisters were hiding, not having bothered to look for them, as his mind was on her alone. Pretending to relent, the clever princess asked that he go and find them so that they could all make the arrangements together. But Riche-Cautèle answered that he did not dare approach the princesses until she was his wife: they would surely exercise their rights as her elders and stand in her way.

Rightly wary of the dastardly prince, Finette felt more suspicious than ever on hearing that answer. She shuddered to think what might have befallen her sisters, and vowed to avenge them with the same ruse by which she would elude the fate she believed they had suffered. To that end, the young princess told Riche-Cautèle she would gladly marry him, but she was convinced that evening weddings always led to unhappy marriages, and so wanted to delay the exchange of vows until the next morning. She promised not to breathe a word of all this to her sisters, then asked to be left alone for a time so that she could do her devotions, after which she would show him to a room with a fine bed, then lock herself into her own room until morning.

Riche-Cautèle was not a brave man. Seeing Finette still brandishing that massive hammer, waving it back and forth like a fan, he decided he would do well to consent, and withdrew to let her meditate for a while. As soon as he was gone, Finette hurried off and laid out a bed over a drain hole in the floor of one of the chateau's rooms. The room was as clean as any other, but all the wastes of the chateau were dumped into that drain, which was extremely wide. Finette laid two very thin planks over the hole, gently placed a mattress atop them, and hurried straight back to her room. Riche-Cautèle reappeared a moment later. The princess led him to the bed she had made up and bade him goodnight. The prince dropped onto the bed fully clothed, and the two thin sticks imme-diately gave way. He fell straight to the bottom of the sewer, suffering twenty bumps on the head and bruises all over his body. The prince's fall made a tremendous racket, and as the drain was not far from Finette's room, she knew at once that her trick had succeeded every bit as well as she hoped, feeling a secret joy that she found very pleasant. No words could describe her exultation on hear-ing him splashing about in the sewer. He deserved that punishment, and the princess was right to be pleased.

But she was not so lost in her pleasure that she forgot her sisters. Her first thought was to go looking for them. Babillarde proved easy to find: after carefully locking her in, Riche-Cautèle had left the key in his room. Finette opened the door; waking with a start at the noise, her sister was stunned to see Finette standing before her. Finette told her how she had got rid of the devious prince who had come to take advantage of them. Her story left Babillarde thunderstruck, for despite all her glib talk she was so blind to the ways of the world she had absurdly believed every-thing Riche-Cautèle had told her. Dupes of that sort can still be found to this day. Choking back her sorrow, she left with Finette to go looking for Nonchalante. They searched every room in the chateau and found no trace of their sister; finally it occurred to Finette that she might be in the garden house, where they did indeed find her, half dead with despair and depletion, for she had taken no food all day long. The princesses gave her all the aid she required, then told her the story that had already brought such mortal sadness to Babillarde. With that they all went off to rest.

As for Riche-Cautèle, he spent a most uncomfortable night, and the dawn brought no great improvement. The prince found himself in a cavern whose full horror he could not see, for daylight never found its way in. Nonetheless, after many struggles, he found the way out: the sewer opened into a river at some distance from the chateau. He managed to draw the attention of a little crowd of fishermen, who pulled him from the water in a state that inspired compassion in their kindly hearts.

He had himself conveyed to his father's court, where he could recover at leisure; there his humiliation filled him with a hatred of Finette so strong that he thought less of healing than of avenging himself.

Meanwhile, the princess was deeply distressed. To her, a good name was a thousand times dearer than life itself, and her sisters' shameful weakness cast her into a despair she could scarcely overcome. Further testing Finette's devotion, her sisters seemed to be in unsteady health after their illegitimate marriages.

Riche-Cautèle had always been quite a scoundrel, but now, fully recovering his wits after his adventure, he became a scoundrel without peer. Neither the sewer nor his injuries aggrieved him as much as the humiliation of having found someone cleverer than he. He suspected that the sisters might be suffering certain after-effects of their marriages; hoping to tempt their appetite, he had enormous crates planted with fruit-laden trees brought to the chateau and left beneath the windows. Nonchalante and Babillarde, who often stood staring outside from those windows, did not fail to see the beautiful fruit and to feel a sudden violent craving; they nagged at Finette to ride down in the basket to pick them some. The good-hearted princess was happy to oblige her sisters. She let herself be lowered to the ground and came back with a load of that delicious fruit, which they greedily devoured.[15]

The next day they saw fruit trees of another kind beneath their windows; again the princesses were tempted, again Finette indulged them, but this time Riche-Cautèle's hidden henchmen did not fail to capture her as they had the day before. They seized hold of Finette and dragged her away before the eyes of her sisters, who tore their hair out in despair.

Riche-Cautèle's men took Finette to a country house where the prince was completing his recovery. Boiling with rage at the princess, he said a hundred brutal things to her, and she answered with an assurance and a strength worthy of the heroine that she was. Finally, after keeping

---

15. Violent and insatiable cravings for fruit were seen as a sign of pregnancy.

her prisoner for a few days, he had her conveyed to the top of a very high mountain, and he followed after. Arriving at the summit, he told her she would be put to death in a manner that would avenge him for the tricks she'd played on him. That barbaric prince showed Finette a barrel studded inside with knives, razors, and hooked nails. As a suitable punishment for her treachery, he told her, she would be thrown into that barrel and rolled down the mountainside all the way to the valley below. Finette was no Roman, but she looked on the torment awaiting her with the coolness of Regulus himself.[16] The young princess remained as collected as ever, and even as quick-witted. Rather than admire her heroic nature, Riche-Cautèle loathed her all the more, and resolved to delay her death no longer. He bent down before the barrel that was to be the instrument of his vengeance, looking inside to be sure it was properly fitted with all his murderous weapons. Seeing her persecutor so absorbed in the examination of that barrel, Finette did not waste a moment: she nimbly pushed him into the barrel and started it rolling down the mountainside before the prince could grasp what was happening. With that she

---

16. Marcus Atilius Regulus was a Roman general who was taken hostage by the Carthaginians at Tunis in 255 BCE. Released on the condition that he return to Rome and urge surrender, he rather advised that the war be continued, then willingly returned to his incarceration and eventual execution in Carthage.

fled, and the prince's servants, who had been deeply troubled by his cruel plans for the adorable princess, made no attempt to hold her back. Besides, they were so horrified at what had just happened to Riche-Cautèle that they could think of nothing other than trying to stop the runaway barrel. But their efforts were in vain: it rolled and bounced all the way to the bottom, where they pulled out their prince riddled with a thousand wounds.

King Moult-Bénin and Prince Bel-à-Voir were distraught to learn of Riche-Cautèle's misfortune, but the king's subjects were not sorry at all; Riche-Cautèle was widely hated, and no one could understand how the good and generous younger prince could so love his detestable brother. But the pure-hearted Bel-à-Voir felt a strong bond to everyone in his family, and Riche-Cautèle always took care to show him such friendship that the good prince would never have forgiven himself for not returning it. And so Bel-à-Voir wept over his brother's wounds, and took every possible step to speed their healing. But even with all the loving care he was given, Riche-Cautèle could not be comforted. On the contrary, his wounds seemed only to fester, and for a long time they left him no peace.

Having saved herself from the horrific threat she had faced, Finette was glad to return to the chateau and her sisters, but she was not there long before new trouble came along: much to Finette's chagrin, her two sisters gave birth to two sons. Still, the young princess's courage did not fail her: determined to conceal her sisters' shame, she came up with a plan—a plan that she knew would expose her to danger again, though she took every measure that prudence can inspire. Dressed as a man, she sealed her sisters' babies in two crates, then made little holes close by their mouths, so that they could breathe. She took a horse and rode off with those crates and several others, soon arriving at the capital of Moult-Bénin's kingdom, where Riche-Cautèle was staying.

Upon her arrival, Finette learned that the generous reward Prince Bel-à-Voir was offering to anyone who might heal his brother had attracted charlatans from all over Europe to the court. For in those days there were many adventurers without title or talent who passed themselves off as great men with a divinely given power to cure all manner of ailments. In truth, their only gift was for brazen deception, but wherever they went, they always found a populace eager to believe in them. They knew how to impress the people with their outward appearance and the bizarre names they took. Such healers never stayed in the place of their birth, and often the simple fact that they came from far away gave them a special prestige in the minds of the common folk.

Well informed of all this, the ingenious princess invented a name that would seem very foreign in that kingdom: Sanatio. She had it publicly announced that good Sir Sanatio had come to town, bringing with him many marvelous secrets to cure all sorts of wounds, no matter how grave or how diseased. Bel-à-Voir sent for Sanatio straight away. Finette played the doctor to perfection, casually letting slip five or six words of the medical art; nothing was missing. She was surprised at Bel-à-Voir's handsome face and agreeable manners. After they had talked for some time, discussing Riche-Cautèle's wounds in detail, she said she would be back with a bottle of very special water; in the meantime, she would leave two crates she had brought, which contained excellent unguents, perfectly suited to the prince's case.

With that the make-believe doctor left, and did not come back. The court waited with mounting impatience; just as a messenger was about to be sent with an urgent summons, the sound of tiny children's cries could be heard coming from Riche-Cautèle's room. Everyone looked around in surprise, for there were no children in sight. Finally, one of the courtiers listened very closely, and it was revealed that the cries were coming from within the doctor's crates.

It was indeed Finette's nephews who were making that noise. The princess had had them well fed before she brought them to the palace, but much time had gone by, and now they wanted more, expressing in their need in plaintive wails. The crates were opened, and to the astonishment of all they held two very pretty little boys. Riche-Cautèle immediately suspected another of Finette's tricks, and fell into a fury beyond all expression; at the same time, his pain grew so terrible that it seemed clear he was doomed.

Bel-à-Voir was overcome with grief, and Riche-Cautèle, perfidious to the last, thought he could take advantage of his brother's tenderness. "You have always loved me, Prince," he said, "and you weep to lose me. I require no further proof of your love. I will not live much longer, but if I was ever truly dear to you, promise me you will carry out one final favor."

Given his brother's condition, Bel-à-Voir felt he could not refuse, and so he most solemnly promised to grant him anything he asked. Hearing these words, Riche-Cautèle embraced his brother and said, "I die a consoled man, Prince, since I will be avenged. For what I ask is that you seek Finette's hand in marriage as soon as I am dead. Her father will no doubt approve of your marriage to that meddlesome princess. Then, once you have her in your power, you will plunge a dagger into her breast." Bel-à-Voir recoiled in horror and repented for his imprudent vow, but there was no taking it back, and he did not want to reveal his regret to his brother, who expired soon after. King Moult-Bénin's grief was great. As for his people, far from lamenting the loss of Riche-Cautèle, they were delighted that his death assured Bel-à-Voir's place on the throne, for his merit was admired and respected by all.

Safely back in the company of her sisters, Finette learned of Riche-Cautèle's death; not long after, it was announced to the three princesses that their father the king had returned. He came straight to their tower, and his first act was to ask to see the glass distaffs. Nonchalante went and got Finette's, showed it to the king, gave him a deep curtsey and took the distaff back. Babillarde played the same trick. When it came her turn, Finette showed him the same distaff, which was genuinely hers. But the king's suspicions were aroused; he wanted to see all three of the distaffs together, and only Finette could produce hers. The king flew into such a rage at his two elder daughters that he sent them straight to the fairy who had given him the distaffs, beseeching her to keep his daughters beside her for as long as they lived, and to punish them as they deserved.

As a first step in their punishment, the fairy led them to a gallery of her enchanted chateau, whose walls were painted with scenes from the lives of a vast succession of women celebrated for their virtue and their industriousness. Through a wondrous effect of fairy magic, every figure in the paintings was endowed with movement, and remained in continual motion from morning to night. On all sides there were trophies and epigrams in honor of these virtuous women, and the sisters were mortified to compare those heroines' triumphs with the deplorable state to which their own imprudence had re-

duced them. To further heighten their sorrow, the fairy
gravely told them that they could have avoided their ignoble fate had they only occupied themselves as well as
the women they saw in the paintings, assuring them that
idleness is *the mother of all vices* and the source of all their
unhappiness. The fairy added that she intended to keep
the sisters very busy, so as to prevent them from ever falling back into disgrace and to ensure that they made up for
all the time they had wasted. She was true to her word,
forcing the princesses to undertake the roughest and low-
est sorts of labors, and sending them out to the garden to
pick peas and pull weeds, without a moment's thought for
their fair complexions. Nonchalante did not have the
strength to endure her despair at living a life so counter to
her inclinations; she died of sorrow and exhaustion. Not
long after, Babillarde managed to escape the fairy's chateau under cover of darkness, but she knocked her head on
a tree and died of that injury, surrounded by peasants.

By her nature a good-hearted soul, Finette was racked
by a cruel grief at her sisters' fate; and then, in the midst of
her sorrow, she learned that Prince Bel-à-Voir had asked
for her hand, and that her father had agreed without telling her, because in those days the wishes of the parties involved were the last thing to be considered in marriage.
Finette trembled on hearing this news; she rightly feared
that Riche-Cautèle's hatred had passed into the heart of
the brother who cherished him, and suspected that the

young prince wanted to marry her only so as to sacrifice her to his brother. Her mind full of that apprehension, the princess went to consult the wise fairy, who esteemed her as deeply as she scorned Nonchalante and Babillarde.

The fairy would tell Finette nothing; she would only say, "Princess, you are wise and prudent; you have always chosen your course of conduct well, for at all times you have remembered that *wariness is the mother of safety.* So long as you keep that maxim in mind, you will find your happiness without the aid of my powers." Failing to extract any clarification from the fairy, Finette returned to the palace in a state of deep foreboding.

A few days later, an ambassador officially wed the princess in Bel-à-Voir's name, whereupon she was taken in a magnificent carriage to join her new husband. The first two villages past the border of Moult-Bénin's kingdom held public celebrations in honor of her inaugural trip to their land; in the third she found Bel-à-Voir, whose father had ordered that he come and meet her. Everyone was mystified by the young prince's visible sadness as he entered into a marriage he had claimed to want; the king himself rebuked him for it, and sent him to meet the princess over his objections.

The moment he laid eyes on her, Bel-à-Voir was left speechless by her charms; he paid her a compliment, but so fumblingly that both courts, well aware of the prince's elegance and wit, concluded her beauty had so moved him that it cost him his presence of mind. The city resounded with cries of joy, and from all around concerts and fireworks could be heard. Finally, after a magnificent supper, it came time to lead the new couple to their room.

Finette had not forgotten the maxim of which the good fairy had reminded her, and so she had already come up with a plan. The princess had gained the loyalty of one of her new maidservants who had the key to their apartments, and had asked her to bring in some straw, a bladder, some sheep's blood, and the bowels of a few of the animals that had been eaten at dinner. The princess invented a pretext to slip away into her room, and there she used the straw to construct a human figure, into which she placed the bowels and the bladder, now filled with blood. She dressed that mannequin in a woman's bonnet and nightgown, then rejoined the festivities; soon after, the princess and her husband were led to their room. Once all the preparations for bed were complete, the principal lady in waiting took away the torches and withdrew. Immediately Finette cast the straw woman into the bed and hid in a corner.

Heartsick, the prince heaved two or three tormented sighs, then duly drew his sword and plunged it deep into the false Finette. He felt the blood spurting out, and saw the woman of straw lying motionless before him. "What have I done?" cried Bel-à-Voir. "After so many sleepless nights! After so long debating the virtue of keeping my vows if it means committing a crime, in the end I have taken the life of a princess I was born to love! Her charms delighted me the moment I saw her, and yet I could not find the strength to cast off a promise obtained through vile trickery by a brother mad with rage! Oh, merciful heavens! Who would ever seek to punish a woman for being too virtuous? Well then, Riche-Cautèle, I have satisfied your criminal vengeance, but now my death will avenge Finette in her turn. Yes, beautiful princess, with this same sword I shall . . ." Finette heard the prince desperately feeling around for his sword, for he had dropped it in his transport of grief. She had guessed his intentions; not wanting him to commit any such foolishness, she cried out, "Prince, I am not dead. I could see that your heart was too good not to repent of your act, and by an innocent deception I have spared you the guilt of a crime."

Finette then revealed her ingenious plan to construct a straw woman. Ecstatic to find the princess still alive, Bel-à-Voir admired her unflagging foresight, and felt infinitely in her debt for having spared him a crime he could not contemplate without horror. He could not understand how he had ever been so weak as to fail to see the illegitimacy of the accursed promise exacted from him under such false pretenses.

Had Finette not always been thoroughly convinced that *wariness is the mother of safety*, then she would have been killed, and her death would have led to Bel-à-Voir's, whereupon the strangeness of the prince's sentiments would have been the talk of the court. Long live prudence and presence of mind! They preserved these two spouses from very dire sorrows, and now offered them the sweetest destiny in the world. They loved each other with all possible tenderness for as long as they lived, happier and more widely respected than we might readily describe.

There, Madame, is the wondrous story of Finette. I will admit that I have elaborated on it, and spun it out a bit in my telling, but to tell stories is to show that one has few occupations, and so one seeks to amuse oneself, harmlessly, I think, by drawing them out to make the conversation last longer. Besides, I believe that most often the true charm of these playful little tales is to be found in their tiny details. Believe me, charming Countess, it is easy to tell them in a quick, abridged form. Whenever you like, I assure you, I will tell you Finette's adventures in very few words. But that is not how the story was told to me as a child; the telling went on for at least a good hour.

I am certain you know that this tale is well known, but I wonder if you have heard what tradition tells us of its antiquity. It is said that the troubadours or storytellers of Provence invented Finette long before Abélard or the famous count Thibaut de Champagne produced their novels.[17] Fables such as this always contain an uplifting moral. You have remarked, very rightly, that it is a very fine idea to recite them to children, so as to inspire a love of virtue. I know not whether you were told of Finette at that age; but as for me,

A hundred and a hundred times more
My nursemaid, spurning all animal fables,
Regaled me with the moral traits
Of that surprising story
In which we find, bedeviled by ill fortune,
A dangerous prince whom a dark force
Led into the horror of vice.
And of course two imprudent princesses
Who spent their days in empty indulgence,
And unworthily fell
Into terrible misdeeds,
Receiving, as the price of their weakness,
A quick, well-deserved punishment.
But even as, in this fine story, we see
Vice punished and defeated,
So do we see the virtuous
Triumphing and covered with glory.
After a thousand changes of fortune

---

17. Abélard was a medieval theologian and philosopher remembered today for his love affair with Héloïse. The thirteenth-century Thibaut de Champagne was king of Navarre and a poet about whom not much is known.

The wise, prudent Finette

And the generous Bel-à-Voir

Live on in glory.

Yes, these tales are far more striking

Than the deeds of the monkey and the fox.

I always took great pleasure in them,

And all children do the same.

But these fables would please even the

    greatest minds

If you, beautiful Countess, would offer them

    the adornment

Of your wonderful talents.

Ancient Gaul calls you to that task:[18]

And so, deign to fill their days

With the naive but ingenious stories

Invented by the troubadours.

The mysterious meaning that their design

    contains

Is as fine as anything we might find in Aesop.[19]

---

18. Though in 1695 Murat had not yet published her *Contes des fées* (*Fairy Tales*) or her *Nouveaux contes de fées* (*New Fairy Tales*), this allusion suggests that she had begun working on them (both would be published in 1698).

19. Aesop was a famed storyteller and fabulist in ancient Greece.

THE WONDERS OF ELOQUENCE;
OR, THE VIRTUES OF A CIVIL TONGUE

To Madame the Duchess of Epernon

So, beautiful Duchess, you wish to interrupt your serious pursuits for a few moments to hear one of those Gallic fables said to come down to us from the once-celebrated storytellers and troubadours of Provence?[1] I know that to minds as great and perfect as yours nothing is without interest, that in the most trivial bagatelle they can find subjects for profound reflection that most would never see; indeed, I cannot help but think that you will come up with just such a reflection on first sight. You will no doubt be surprised, you whom the deepest ideas have never surprised, that these tales, farfetched as they

---

1. L'héritier is inscribing this story into the oral French tradition of medieval storytellers, a move that underscores her position in the quarrel of the ancients and the moderns by building up France's homegrown mythological tradition rather than borrow from the classical repertoire. For more on this polemical debate, see Seifert and Stanton (Introduction). By underscoring the oral transmission of the story, L'héritier shrewdly speaks to its authenticity, positioning herself as storyteller rather than author and, as readers will later see, as objective historian.

are, have survived the ages without anyone troubling to write them down:

> They are not easy to believe,
> But so long as there are children in this world,
> And mothers, and grandmothers,
> Their memory will live on.[2]

I was told this story as a child, by a lady with a fine knowledge of ancient Greece and Rome, and even more of ancient Gaul; she sought to plant in my head the notion that it harms no one to be polite, or, to put it as the old proverb does, "Kind words burn no tongue," and often

> Sweet and thoughtful language
> Is worth more than a bountiful inheritance.

She tried to prove the truth of that maxim—a very wise maxim, Gothic though it be—by the wondrous story I would now like to tell you.

In the days when France was home to fairies, ogres, sprites, and other such beings (it is difficult to give a precise date, but no matter), there was a respected gentleman who passionately loved his wife (and for that reason too I cannot begin to imagine when this might have

---

2. These are the last four lines of Charles Perrault's fairy tale in verse "Peau d'âne," usually translated as "Donkeyskin" (157).

been).[3] His wife loved him no less; he was a good man, and he well deserved her love. They lived happily for fifteen or sixteen years, but then death separated them forever. The woman died, leaving only a daughter.

The mother was a beautiful creature, and so was her daughter, graced with a thousand charms even as a child. Her skin was so dazzlingly fair that she came to be known by all as Blanche.

Her mother had no money; the father had once been a rich man, but by the time his wife died he had lost everything, for his business affairs did not prosper during their marriage. The only dowry his daughter could offer was her beauty and her white skin, which is most often of little help when it comes time to seek an advantageous match.

Deeply afflicted by his wife's death, her father believed he would never find consolation until he married again. Thinking his daughter young enough that he needn't hurry to find her a husband, he resolved to think of himself first and began to consider his choices. Given the lamentable state of his finances, he was inclined to seek wealth above all, and so he entered into a liaison with a widow who was neither young nor beautiful but was possessed of a sizable fortune.

---

3. L'héritier, like many other *conteuses*, picks up the theme of disillusionment in love and marriage.

This woman, like him childless other than a daughter, was the widow of a financier who had successfully used every trick of his trade to scale the summits of wealth. The financier and his wife were of equal birth, and so no question of rank or honor ever came between them, but as she clung to the ways and the thinking of her family, she had raised her child as she had been brought up herself; and—the girl being of a naturally crude character, easily influenced by bad examples—one can scarcely imagine two more common and vulgar people than that mother and daughter. True to their nature, they were consumed by an excessive but ignorant ambition: they had ideas so ridiculous that they committed a hundred absurdities in which the foolishness they had contracted from their luxurious life and their vanity was all too plain to see.

Given the widow's turn of mind, it should come as no surprise that she warmly welcomed Blanche's father's proposal—he was after all a marquis—and that her hunger for a noble name brought her to the altar just a few days later. Her new husband had imagined that only good things would come of their marriage; once the wedding was over, he was dismayed to discover just how numerous and vexatious were the failings of the marquise he had created. But he was always inclined to avoid strife at all costs, and since it was his nature to let himself be ruled by his wife, such as she was, he lived with her happily enough so long as he never contradicted her and let her be the unquestioned authority in all things. He consoled himself for her difficult temper with the pleasures he derived from the great fortune she brought him; he stoically endured her fits of rage, and whenever he'd had enough of her shrieking and bellowing, since he was a man who loved books, he went off to read in his private study.

Only the good Blanche was wholly deserving of pity. Her stepmother felt an inconceivable loathing for the girl, enraged that Blanche's beauty underscored her daughter's ugliness and made her an object of scorn all around, for Alix (as the girl was named) was as repellently ugly as she was uncouth. Nonetheless, her mother loved her as she was, to the point of idolatry: she would have sacrificed anything for her daughter's pleasure. To further heighten Blanche's sorrows, Alix hated her a hundred times more than her mother did. She used every imaginable means to torment her. The mother wanted Blanche placed in a convent, but Alix, realizing that she could make Blanche a victim of her caprices forever, talked her mother out of it: once Blanche was free of them she might find some helpful friend who could show her to her best advantage and find her a rich, dazzling husband, and that was something Alix feared more than death itself.

And so it was decided that Blanche would stay with the family, and never go visiting, and never receive guests.

They took steps to hide her from all people of quality, and to spoil her beauty they forced her to handle the chores of the chambermaids, the charwomen, even the cooks.

Madame, if I wanted to tell you this tale just as the Provençal storytellers taught it to our grandmothers, I would list a thousand astonishing traits of Blanche's skill, but there is no need for such things. I will tell you only that, with an admirable docility very rare in such a lovely young woman, she readily accepted the unpleasant tasks her stepmother assigned her, bringing a fresh luster to everything she touched, showing an unparalleled talent for pleating a ruff or pressing a high collar. She did all this so deftly that if she were living today I have no doubt that she would know just how to fashion a *rayon*[4] and would attract a great court among the multitude of women who are continually mortified that their stubborn *rayon* refuses to stay in place, despite all the trouble they take to set it just so. Blanche would give that ornament—so useful for the beautiful ladies of the land of the pygmies[5]—a perfect symmetry, outshining even Mme

---

4. A hairstyle, with hair piled on the top of the head, popular at the end of the seventeenth century ("Rayon").

5. The legend of a tribe of short-statured people living somewhere in Africa or perhaps India dates back at least to Homer's *Iliad*; the name derives from a Greek word for the measurement from elbow to fingertip, an approximation of a such a person's height. That notion took root in the European imagination (no doubt in part because it relies on a sense of the otherness and therefore the inferiority of the non-European); by the time of these stories, "the land of the pygmies" was a well-worn cliché.

D***, with whom no coquette dares to quarrel, as she has the admirable talent of coiffing herself better, and of arranging a *cornette* better,[6] than all the professional hairdressers in the universe. That tremendous advantage has earned her the admiration and complaisance of a great many women, for she is generous with her talents, and can make their heads just as perfect as her own. But enough of that; let us return to our story.

Not only did they inflict a thousand wearinesses on Blanche; they also took care to keep her so wretchedly dressed that she would have looked a slattern were it not for her natural ability to seem fresh and dainty no matter how she was attired. They tried to give her clothes that would spoil her beauty, but in fact they only brought it out: even uncombed and dressed in rough serge, she was as beautiful as Love itself, whereas Alix, covered in gold and precious gems, and with the most elaborate hairdo imaginable, frightened everyone who looked at her, for her excessive adornments made her seem all the cruder and uglier. Nonetheless, she refused to closet herself away at home. She showed herself off at every promenade, every spectacle, every ball; she never wearied of flaunting her finery, but while she found some pleasure in attracting the gaze of an occasional bourgeoise, she was stung

---

6. Reference to a hairstyle that women wore in their private chambers ("Cornette").

to hear the hurtful truths spoken behind her back by the pages or musketeers of that century, for in those days, many musketeers, minor officers, riding academy students, and other young fools had a most ridiculous habit: whenever they came across a woman sporting any sort of finery, they made a great show of inspecting her, then assailed her with a thousand impertinences if they did not find her beautiful enough for their liking. We can easily imagine how those young boors exercised their gift for heartless mockery when they saw Alix's repugnant face, but what we would less readily guess is that she avenged herself for those insults on Blanche. Supposing that her ugliness would not have to endure such disdain if there were no beautiful women in the world, she conceived an even greater hatred for the good-hearted Blanche, and encouraged her mother to heap yet more miseries upon her.

In spite of Blanche's natural gentleness, her mistreatment sometimes so embittered her that she dreamt of fleeing that house with a great clamor; but her natural dislike of scandal, her love for her father, and her hope of finding some opportunity to cast off her slavery without conflict dissuaded her from making a tumultuous exit. Once again, then, she armed herself with patience, and her father, who deeply loved her but lacked the firmness to oppose her barbaric treatment, eased her sorrows by sharing them, praising her virtues, comforting her with the promise of a happier place, one day, in heaven. These consolations kept Blanche in that house despite her unhappiness; and although she was forbidden all company and any sort of diversion, she found a way to have them all the same, by retiring to her room and reading. She amassed a great many novels, I do not know how, but she could not draw from them all the pleasure they held, for she could read only at night, her stepmother relentlessly keeping her busy all through the day. She could only find time to read by going without sleep, but that did not stop her: to her reading felt like sweet repose, and whenever she could steal a few moments during the day, she hurried back to her books.

Her stepmother kept a close watch on her, and she was indignant to see Blanche so often retreating to the solitude of her room. Wanting to know what attracted her there so powerfully, she caught her one day as she was lost in one of the finest passages of a novel as admirably written as it was pleasingly devised. The marquise should have been touched to see the innocent distraction that was poor Blanche's only solace, but instead she who could scarcely read threw herself on the book, ripped it from Blanche's hands, and after with great difficulty deciphering the title—for it was a complicated Greek name that she could scarcely pronounce—she finally grasped that the book was a novel. She was just launching into a terrible tantrum when, fortunately for the girl, her father entered. Before he could speak a word, his wife shrieked at him, "So, Monsieur fancy-pants, with all your high-flown talk, so this is how you raise your hag of a daughter? I've just caught her secretly reading a love story!"

As it happened, the Marquis was feeling a little braver than usual that day, and so, inspecting the book, he answered his wife, "Blanche is quite right to find distraction in reading. You have robbed her of all her pleasures; she cannot do better than to seek out a new one, one that has much to teach both her mind and her manners. I am always glad to see daughters of good family spend their time reading. If only they would all take it up! Then we would not see them so lost when it comes to occupying their leisure; they would not run as they do from one public show to another, or waste their days in the gambling house."

Knowing well that her daughter was as drawn to gambling as she was to every other sort of pleasure, the Marquise took those words as a veiled attack on Alix. Raising her voice still further, she shot back, "Why, if I didn't know better I'd think a certain someone was trying to forbid women of quality, with a fortune in the thousands, from entertaining themselves as they please! The foul brats of a penniless nobility may deserve to have those pleasures forbidden them, but a woman with more pistoles than those trollops have deniers can do as she likes.[7] As for young ladies without a sou to their name, all they need is to know how to do housework, and devote themselves to it all day long; if they must play at being readers, let it at least be with decent books, not the sort where you learn all kinds of wickedness."[8]

"One does not learn wickedness in the fine novels I see my daughter read," answered Blanche's father, for he had once read them even more eagerly than she, and he enjoyed them still. "On the contrary, one finds only noble sentiments, only fine examples: vice is always punished, and virtue rewarded. Indeed, I might go so far as to say that for the very young, novels are in a sense more suitable even than history, since history is wholly enslaved to the truth and thus sometimes portrays images of the most shocking immorality. History shows us men as they are, novels as they should be, and so urge us to aspire to perfection; at the very least, it cannot be denied that a well-written novel teaches the ways of society and the proper use of language. Blanche is already a fine, gracious speaker, and I hope that the reading of these pleasant works will perfect that talent."

---

7. A pistole was a coin of considerable value, worth ten French livres, or pounds. (The value of a livre is equivalent to a pound of silver, or a little over two hundred contemporary dollars.) A denier, on the other hand, was worth very little, only 1/240th of a pound. A sou, referred to in the next sentence, was worth 1/20th of a pound.

8. The stepmother is drawing on the notion, which gained popularity during the rise of the novel, that girls and women would be corrupted by the immorality and scandal purportedly promoted in such texts.

The stepmother, who understood not one word of his argument, and who was by nature a joyless and closed-minded creature, did not intend to relent in her harsh treatment of Blanche; she would not allow the marquis to complete his paean to reading, though he was perfectly prepared to go on, for he was a master at that subject.

"Will you listen to this man blather on!" she cried. "Ye gods! All right, then, let your daughter read her fill, since that little game pleases her and you, but if she slacks off on the housekeeping I know how to put her back to work."

And she stormed off, putting an end to this edifying conversation.

Perhaps, Madame, you will think that Blanche's father was a bit overfond of novels, you who occupy yourself with only the most sublime readings; I know not what you may think of all this, nor will I offer my opinion: I am simply telling you what I find in my chronicle. I am a historian, and a historian, man or woman, must not take sides. Do not make light of these considerations, I beg you, for if you were to lose your seriousness then I would lose mine in turn, and I need every bit of it if I am to tranquilly tell you the next episode of this extraordinary story.

Blanche's father was not wrong; his beautiful daughter's natural sweetness was soon augmented by an informed, subtle sense of the social niceties. One could not express oneself more pleasantly and more precisely than she came to do, whether through her engagement with the inventions of the human mind or from some other source. Neither Alix nor her mother envied her new talents; they were too coarse to perceive the delicacy of the things they heard her say, so they went on resenting only her physical charms and dreamt more than ever of taking them from her.

When summer came, the Marquis and his family set off for the country, where Blanche's stepmother exercised to the utmost her gift for tormenting the girl. She burdened her with the most arduous chores, bur despite her insistence on exposing Blanche to the sun at all times, her naturally fair skin remained as white as ever. Her stepmother was consumed with spite to see that nothing could make the girl ugly, and she could not drive that goal from her mind. Finally, after all else had failed, she resolved to add to her duties the task of fetching the entire household's water from a distant fountain.

Blanche patiently endured her fate, and she did not rebel against this new order any more than she did at her usual duties; fetching water was no more humiliating a task than a hundred others she was assigned. Indeed, she saw other young women going to that same fountain, for the customs of that time were in some ways very different from today, and she might have found solace in their example if she had been going there of her own will, like these young countrywomen, or because her father was too poor to hire a servant. But, patient and stoical though she was, she could scarcely hold back her tears when she reflected that these exhausting labors were forced on her only for the purpose of defeating her spirit and blighting her beauty. That was her one sorrow, for not only did she have the example of her neighbor women, but she had also read that the daughters of kings did the washing in Homer's time, and that Achilles himself was a very able cook.[9] And so, without having to be asked, Blanche went off to fetch water whenever it was needed.

That fountain was surrounded by the most beautiful countryside in the world, but it was a dangerous place to linger, for not far away was a forest full of wolves that often passed by on their rounds; a discreet rumor had it that this was precisely why Blanche's stepmother was so bent on sending her there. Several times that sweet girl was warned of the danger she faced, but even if the wolves were not what she feared most, those warnings could do her no good, for her stepmother implacably refused to see sense.

After she had gone to the fountain several times and seen neither man nor beast, as my author puts it, one day she had just filled her jug when she spied a wild boar racing furiously toward her, though she saw no one chasing it. Poor Blanche shrieked in terror; one might rightly take fright at far less, Madame. But she was not so afraid

---

9. Allusion to Homer's *Odyssey* (6.1–110) and *Iliad* (9.195–220).

that she didn't think of protecting herself; she took to her heels, and she was already nearing the cover of the bushes when a sharp blow to her shoulder sent her tumbling to the ground. At the same moment, the boar brushed harmlessly past and took cover in the woods. Painfully struggling to stand, she heard someone call out, "My beautiful child, I've hurt you! I was aiming for the boar! Oh, woe is me!" Raising her eyes, Blanche saw a richly dressed young man coming forward to help her up. Although she was very pale from loss of blood, the hunter saw with one glance that she was an extraordinarily beautiful young woman, and he was moved by the sweet, winsome air he found in her, despite the plainness of her attire. But he wasted no time in compliments, for he was a man of sound judgment, and his first thought was to come to her aid. He ripped up his handkerchief, and even his cravat—or his ruff, if you prefer—to stanch the blood from her wound. The story tells us that Blanche's eyes wounded the hunter in their turn, but I doubt that could have happened so quickly; if the chronicle tells the truth, then that hunter must have been as easily ignited as his rifle.

Here some critic is bound to object that the hunter had no rifle, since artillery was unknown in the days of the fairies. I know scholars so scrupulous that they cannot hear a story out without venting their indignation at such anachronisms, but if I wanted to argue with such a senseless censor, could I not tell him that Mesdames the fairies might simply have been playing one of their little tricks? Many other marvels will be seen; this one was well within their grasp, especially as a service to the hunter in question, for he was the godson of Mélusine, of Logistille, of I know not how many others, of all the most celebrated of those helpful creatures.[10]

But it is indeed true that the weapon by which Blanche was wounded was no firearm[11] (for a historian must always tell the truth, though I know a great many who do not); rather, it was a lance or a javelin that the prince had hurled at the boar . . . But I believe I have not yet told you that this hunter was a prince? Well, no matter; I will recount what I know of his genealogy later. For the moment, I must return to poor Blanche, whom we have left too long half-conscious on the grass.

Finding herself in the hands of such a surgeon, her fear and uncertainty tortured her as cruelly as the wound she had suffered. The hunter gave her all the aid he could think of, but he was so full of wonder and remorse that he could not speak a word. Finally, having bandaged Blanche's wound as best he could and splashed her face

---

10. In European folklore, Mélusine is a water spirit who is usually represented as a fish or serpent from the waist down. The fairy Logistille is a character in Ludovico Ariosto's *Orlando furioso*.

11. Handheld firearms were introduced in France in the sixteenth century.

with water ten or twelve times, until she no longer seemed in danger of fainting away, the young stranger said to her, "How great are my sorrow and joy today! What a joy to have encountered so charming a person! What a sorrow to have caused her such pain!"

"You caused that pain innocently," answered Blanche, "and so, my Lord, such a sorrow does not deserve to trouble your peace of mind."

"Even if you were an ordinary girl," the stranger replied, "I would be deeply ashamed to have wounded you. Imagine my despair at this accident, then, seeing you as lovely as you are."

"Leaving your flattery to one side," said Blanche, "I must tell you, my Lord, that you push consideration and kindness too far. Had you killed me, the blame would have been with fate, not with you. In any case, so little is lost with the life of a girl such as I—nothing that would deserve to trouble a life like yours, which I believe must be one of those fine lives so useful to the state that, I assure you, people like me would gladly sacrifice their insignificant being to save the precious existence of gentlemen as vital to the public good as you seem to be. And so, my lord, grant me the favor I seek of you, which is that you not rebuke yourself for this incident, for I would only chide myself for the sorrow it gave you."

On first seeing Blanche's attire, the stranger had taken her for a peasant girl, or at best a villager; great was his surprise, then, on hearing the elegance of her speech, but her sweet manner stirred him even more than her refined words. That young prince had a most violent temper, and he knew full well that if someone had even innocently caused him such pain as he had just inflicted on this beautiful young woman, nothing would have contained his violent fury at the culprit. The less capable he was of Blanche's moderation, the more he admired it; with that, then she became the absolute mistress of his soul. Long before Quinault,[12] we see here a fine proof of one of that master's maxims, which so rightly tells us that

> It is beauty that first works to please,
> But a gentle manner makes the charm complete.

The prince was so enchanted that the teeming thoughts in his mind reduced him to silence for a few moments; he broke that silence only to speak a hundred more ardent words to Blanche. But he did not reveal the deep impression she had made on his heart, fearing he might alarm a beautiful young lady whose conversation displayed as much modesty as it did grace and education.

Meanwhile, the prince was deeply troubled to see that his servants had not come to join him. He had wandered off in the hunt, and he was irked that no one had found

---

12. The citation by Philippe Quinault appears in the 1671 miscellany *Psiché*, to which Molière and Pierre Corneille also contributed (Molière et al.).

him, for he wanted to send at once for a coach to take Blanche wherever she might like to go. But when he told her of his concern and his intention, she answered, "My lord, I implore you to give no such orders, and if you have as much consideration for me as you have shown, I assure you that you can give me no greater pleasure than by leaving me to myself without another thought, and telling no one of our meeting or my injury. I have the most powerful reasons in the world for making this request; my only wish is to quietly return to my father's house, once I have rested just a bit more."

After a few sweet words of protest, the prince finally told her, "Very well, then, such is your pleasure, and I will do as you say; but as for not thinking of you, do not believe, my lovely lady, that anyone could obey you in that." With this he took his leave and mounted his horse, while Blanche stayed behind, shaken, weak, and terrified to think what those at home must be thinking after finding her gone for so long.

Finally she rose and set off in great pain to her father's house, arriving just as he was about to send a servant to see what was keeping her. Her stepmother immediately let fly a string of recriminations, but when Blanche answered that an accident had befallen her, that she had been injured by a wild boar and would have died on the spot were it not for a passerby who came to her aid, then her stepmother had no choice but to hold her tongue.

Deeply upset by this news, the marquis ran to his daughter and had her put straight to bed, resolving not to rely on his wife for her care. Now that that dear girl is in good hands, let us return to the prince and his lineage.

He was an ally of Urgande, a cousin of Maugis, a grandnephew of Merlin, and at the same time the god-son of the sage Lirgandée and all the wisest fairies, as I've already told you.[13] Beyond that, no one quite knows of what country he was the future king; some accounts call him the son of a Duke of Normandy, others claim it was the Duke of Brittany, while still others insist that it was the Count of Poitiers who had given him life. This uncertainty derives from the fact that no one has any idea of the site of the fountain where Blanche went to fetch water. In the end, it matters little; it is enough that every account agrees that the hunter who wounded the girl was the son and heir of the sovereign of that land.

The young prince could not drive the memory of that adventure from his mind; as soon as he had found his way back to the hunting party, he ordered one of his most resourceful squires to go to the village and learn what he could of Blanche's life. The squire adroitly carried

---

13. L'héritier is alluding to fairies, wizards, and wise men from many corners of the folkloric tradition: Urgande is a sorceress in the chivalric romance *Amadis de Gaule*; Maugis is another medieval enchanter in the eponymous chanson de geste *Maugis d'Aigrement*; Merlin is the famed wizard in the Arthurian tradition; and Lirgandée—difficult to trace—may be a learned historian and scientist in Cervantes's *Don Quixote*.

out his mission, and gave his master an exact account of that young beauty's birth, tastes, and hardships. The prince was delighted to learn that she came from an illustrious noble family, and considered the steps he would now have to take to ensure the happiness of a woman he thought in every way worthy of it.

Blanche was much loved in the village, as much as Alix was hated, so the peasants told the squire a hundred amusing stories concerning the fine qualities of the one and the shocking defects of the other. Sharp and quick-minded, that gentleman forgot none of the things he had been told, and he recounted them to the prince word for word, with a simplicity that could only move the heart of a lover as absorbed in his amorous thoughts as the hero of a novel.

The prince's first concern was to heal Blanche of the wound he had caused her. Come though he did from a family well versed in the fairy arts, he had no great skill in that domain, and so paid a call on one of his godmothers to tell her of all that had happened. He made no mention of his newfound love for Blanche; he simply asked that the girl be cured. But so ardent was his plea, and so excessive his praise of her merits, that any woman with some experience of life—even a mortal with no knowledge of necromancy—could have easily guessed that he was in love. The good fairy saw it at once, then, and since she genuinely loved her godson she was glad that he had placed this matter in her hands; she was eager to see Blanche and to determine whether she was worthy of the sentiments she had inspired in a heart heretofore impervious to affection.

Dulcicula, for such was this fairy's name,[14] thus went off and prepared a miraculous balm that healed the gravest wounds in less than twenty-four hours. Then she adopted the face of an old peasant woman and knocked at Blanche's father's door. The first person she met was Alix, whom she told, very civilly and in the style of a villager, that she possessed a wonderful secret and had come to offer the marquis her services for his daughter's care.

"What is this madwoman babbling about?" Alix answered irately. "You'd think every hick in this burgh has decided they're going to play nursemaid to that little drudge Blanche; I can't imagine what's the matter with them, getting so worked up and running around like lunatics. That creature's going to wind up just another lump in the graveyard; if she were a good old shepherd dog, she'd be dead already."

Dulcicula was greatly surprised to see this young lady clad in gold and gemstones speaking such curious jargon; but the fairy, who was sweetness itself, was more offended by her heartlessness than by her vulgarity. She did not answer that brute; having learned that the

---

14. A Latin name, rather than a French one: "little sweet one."

marquis was not in, she spoke to a woman he had charged with Blanche's care, who led the fairy to the patient's bed. Still taking care to speak in terms that suited her appearance, Dulcicula told Blanche that she was sorry to hear of her accident, and had come specially from her village to offer her a balm that could quickly cure all manner of injuries.

Blanche was a sensible young woman; she did not scorn the naive beliefs of the local folk, but she felt certain that the balm in question was one of those nostrums that the people place great faith in and refer to as "innocent little cures" because one must be very innocent indeed to rely on them. Nonetheless, true to her character, she amiably answered the fairy, "You're very kind, my good woman, to abandon all your occupations to come here just for my sake; I don't know how to repay you for your solicitude, I who am scarcely in a condition to do as I would like, but I will speak of you to my father, and I hope that he will remember your thoughtfulness. As for the balm, I thank you, but I am currently in the hands of the surgeons, and the treatment must not be changed from one day to the next."

Charmed by Blanche's quietly forthright manner, Dulcicula did not fail to see the girl's low opinion of her balm, but she so ardently pressed her to use it that Blanche finally consented, simply out of a desire to please this woman who seemed so intent on helping her. The fairy put her enchanted balm on the wound, and no sooner had it touched her skin than beautiful Blanche's pain miraculously began to subside.

With that, they fell into conversation. Dulcicula marveled to see such good-heartedness and other fine qualities in one so beautiful, and her admiration had a happy consequence. Clasped in the fairy's hand was a stick that seemed to serve as a cane, but in fact it was the magic wand by which she worked all the wonders of her art. She touched Blanche with that stick, as if by accident, and thereby gave her the gift of being forever even sweeter, more lovable, and more considerate than she was, and with it the most melodious voice in the world. Then she left the beautiful patient's room, accompanied by Blanche's nurse.

The fairy put that nurse onto the subject of Alix, and learned that the harridan was as vain as she was ugly and mean, and that, since she was always dressed in glittering finery, and was forever pulling faces and striking graceless poses in hopes of making herself attractive, she was everywhere referred to ironically as *the lovely Alix*, and in a thousand places, when someone saw a girl putting on affected, impertinent airs, they said she *was playing the lovely Alix*.

Thus informed, the fairy met up again with the very one who had just been so glowingly described to her. Alix was alone in the courtyard; the fairy approached her and politely asked, "Mademoiselle, would you be so good as to tell me where I might find this house's back gate?"

Alix erupted, "Has there ever been anyone in this world as clueless as this doddering old bag who keeps appearing out of nowhere and pestering me with her moronic questions?"

The fairy made no reply, but began to follow after Alix. Touching her with the stick as if by chance, she gave her the gift of being forever furious, unpleasant, and hard—in short, of remaining forever just as she was. Alix flew into such a rage at that wayward stick that she nearly beat the good peasant woman; she did not, but she vomited up a torrent of insults, and the fairy, whose work was done, withdrew.

Meanwhile Blanche, her pain easing since the administration of the magical balm, thought back over the events in the woods. The hunter's handsome face and pleasant manner vividly presented themselves to her mind, and she believed that in all the novels she'd read she had never seen anything as splendid as that incident. She desperately wanted to know who that hunter was, but all those thoughts were born purely of curiosity and gratitude, nothing more. I beg you not to believe that any other sentiment played a role in all this; you would be doing a disservice to Blanche.

As for the prince, he had abandoned himself entirely to his love for Blanche. Dulcicula's description of her merits fanned his fires; he was in such a state that, were it not for his fear of his father the duke, he would have rushed straight off to find that poor beauty and bring her back to the palace in triumph; but, knowing he had no choice, he tried to rein in his ardor, not without a hundred times asking himself how he could possibly manage it.

After twenty hours, just as the old woman had said, Blanche was perfectly healed, and a few days later her pitiless stepmother sent her back to the fountain as if nothing had happened. She was about to draw water when she saw a woman approach, even more remarkable for her grand manner and her grace than for her gown, although she was dressed in a manner as regal as it was coquettish. The lady came to Blanche and said to her:

"My beautiful child, would you be so kind as to give me a drink?"

"Madame," Blanche answered pleasantly, "I am terribly embarrassed that I can only offer it to you in this jug, which is scarcely convenient for drinking."

As she spoke, the girl leaned over the edge of the fountain, carefully rinsed the jug, and then graciously handed it to the lady, who took a drink and gave Blanche her most cordial thanks. She found this young woman so appealing in her ways that her words of gratitude led to a conversation, touching on a thousand pleasant, refined subjects that never left Blanche at a loss for words; the girl answered so intelligently, so amiably, and so thoughtfully that she thoroughly charmed the good stranger before her.

I suspect you have already surmised that this woman was another fairy; what you will not have guessed is that her name was Eloquentia Nativa.[15] That name will be Greek to some, but you, charming Duchess, will have grasped at once that it is quite Latin. But Latin or Greek, it makes no difference, the fairy was indeed known by that fantastical sobriquet, and we should not be surprised: fairies have always had the most curious names. Eloquentia Nativa, then, her mind filled with Blanche's eloquence and engaging manners, resolved to repay her handsomely for the small pleasure she had so openheartedly offered her. The wise fairy placed her hand on Blanche's head and gave her this gift: with every sentence she spoke a stream of pearls, diamonds, rubies, and emeralds would pour from her mouth. With that the fairy said farewell to sweet Blanche, who tranquilly set off for home with her jug of water.

No sooner had Blanche walked in the door than her outraged stepmother demanded to know what had kept her so long at the fountain.

"I came across the most delightful woman I've ever met," answered Blanche.

On those words, a dazzling rain of pearls and gems streamed from her mouth.

"What's this?" cried the marquise.

---

15. That is, "innate eloquence."

Openly and eloquently, Blanche recounted her meeting with the lady and the conversation that ensued, but with every sentence she spoke, even the shortest, a rain more precious than the rain that conquered Danaé fell from her mouth.[16] Everyone hurried to pick up what Blanche was casting forth from her mouth; no one recoiled if some drop of liquid flew from her lips as she spoke, but rather hurried to collect it and preserve it with great care. Blanche cared nothing for riches, but little by little she took to speaking in short sentences. The Marquis's joy was beyond description, which is why I will say nothing of it.

As astonished as she was dismayed, his wife resolved the next day to send Alix to the fountain, in the belief that she too would meet this mysterious woman and would be favored with the same gift as Blanche. People then were just as they are today: forever thinking too much of themselves, wanting wonderful things to happen to them without doing anything to deserve it. She revealed her plan to Alix, who, more boorish than ever, tartly answered that fetching water was no job for a fine girl like her: her mother had to be out of her mind just to speak of it, and she could count her out. But her mother would not let the matter drop, insisting that she was

---

16. Danaé: allusion to Zeus's impregnation of Danaë by flowing into her house in the form of a golden rain.

sending her there for her own good. Finally Alix resigned herself and made ready to go, still spouting a thousand idiocies.

She dressed and adorned herself as carefully as if she were bound for the ball, then picked up a golden ewer, the most beautiful in the house; thus opulently equipped, she made her way to the fountain. Eloquentia Nativa was indeed there beside its waters; the wise fairy had discovered that beautiful, solitary spot not long before, and found it greatly to her liking, but on this day she had taken on the guise of a cheerful peasant woman, with an innocent air and rustic attire, for Eloquentia Nativa was just as beautiful simply dressed as she was draped in the most glittering ornaments. Indeed, when she put on such baubles, her beauty was only diminished.

Alix sat down on the rim of the fountain, and the pretty peasant woman drew near, thirsty after her long walk. Alix's base mind could only be impressed by the glamor of luxurious dress; that alone did she respect, to the extent that she was capable of respect. Alix glared at the woman, not deigning to honor her with a nod, despite the deep curtsey Eloquentia Nativa had given her. But the fairy did not let that put her off; curtseying again, she said to Alix, "Mademoiselle, would you be so kind as to allow me to use your vase to draw water? I am so terribly thirsty."

"Will you listen to this peon!" answered Alix, enraged. "So I suppose people come here just for the pleasure of giving her a drink! And she demands a golden ewer to stick her filthy snout into! Off with you, guttersnipe, and keep your back turned. If you want water, you can drink from our cattle trough."

"You're very brusque, Mademoiselle," the fairy answered. "Have I done something to offend you, that you should treat me this way?"

Alix leapt to her feet, hands on her hips, and bellowed at the stranger, "You seem to be itching for an argument, you wretched trull, but I would advise you to keep your words out of my ears, because I could have you beaten to a pulp the next time you walk past our front door."

Indignant at that creature's brutality, the good fairy resolved to punish her then and there, such that the girl would always remember in horror the insolent torrent unleashed by her venomous tongue. She knocked Alix to the ground with a tap of her stick, and there she gave her the gift, or rather the curse, that with every word she spoke her mouth would disgorge toads, snakes, and spiders, along with other horrid beasts whose poison makes all of humanity shudder. And then Eloquentia Nativa immediately went on her way, leaving the furious Alix behind her.

That vicious young woman waited hours for the magnificent lady and her favors; seeing that her wait would be fruitless, she gave up and went home. Her mother was burning with impatience to see her again, and as soon as she spotted her from the doorway the marquise went to meet her.

"Well!" she said. "Did you meet anyone nice?"

"Oh, yes indeed!" said Alix. "Thank you ever so much for forcing me to go waste my time hanging around that worthless fountain!"

With these words, a pile of snakes, toads, and mice dropped from Alix's mouth.

"Where did that come from, you wretched girl?" cried her mother.

Alix tried to answer; another deluge of vermin ensued. Mother and daughter went inside, where it soon became clear that Alix's fine gift was an illness without cure, and everyone conceived the most complete and utter repugnance for the ignoble girl, an aversion her mother could not help but share.

Meanwhile, ever attentive to anything related to Blanche's existence, the prince soon learned of the happy gift she had received from a fairy; knowing of the power and generosity of Eloquentia Nativa, who was yet another of his godmothers, he suspected that it was she who had worked that wonder. On the pretext of wanting to witness her gift for himself, he displayed a great eagerness to see Blanche come to the court, and went to ask Eloquentia to please find the beautiful girl who was capable of such marvels.

"Did you know," the fairy asked him with a smile, "that those marvels are my own handiwork?"

"No," answered the prince, "but I thank you a thousand times, for I am deeply in love with that young beauty."

"You know I always like to oblige you," the fairy answered, "but you must not thank me for that; I did not know of your passion for Blanche, and you played no part in what I did for her. I was charmed by her sweetness and good manners; her conversation is admirable in every way. Nothing can match her gift for a fine turn of phrase, and so I wanted pearls and gems to pour from her mouth to express the beauty and brilliance I found in her words."

The prince was delighted to hear Blanche's eloquence praised by a fairy whose taste and talent he esteemed a thousand times more than any rule of rhetoric.

Finally Eloquentia Nativa left her godson and made for Blanche's father's chateau. She found it besieged by a throng of incredible size: the glittering things that emerged from Blanche's mouth attracted even more people than the gems produced by the mouth of Monsieur de ***, marvelous though they be.[17] The crowd was entirely right: was it not far more pleasant to see precious stones coming from a pretty little mouth like

---

17. It is not clear to whom L'héritier is referring here, but it is evident that Blanche has gained a place in the rhetorical tradition of orators. For more on this subject, see Seifert (95–96).

Blanche's than to watch lightning bolts emerge from the enormous mouth of that thundering orator so revered by the Athenians?[18]

To the great regret of the crowd gathered around Blanche, Eloquentia invited her to climb into her carriage and took her off to the court. There the prince revealed the devoted, tender feelings he felt for her; Blanche was not unmoved, and as the happy gift that beautiful woman enjoyed made her richer than the loftiest princesses in the universe, the prince married her with the enthusiastic support of his father, the duke, and of all the people of his realms.

Blanche's ecstatic father was greatly esteemed at the court and no longer had to endure his wife's caprices; no longer did she dare nag at him, now that his daughter had scaled such a height. The envious Alix, who habitually tumbled into despair at the mere thought of Blanche being happy, now suffered the new misery of finding that neither her mother nor anyone else could bear having her near. She left her mother's house in a rage and wandered from province to province, where she was an object of loathing for all, and where she experienced all the rigors of poverty! Finally, after many atrocious

---

18. The reference here is to Pericles, a renowned Greek orator of the fifth century BCE; Aristophanes describes Pericles as able to stun all of Greece with the lightning and thunder of his words.

sufferings, she died of indigence *round the back of a bush*,[19] as Blanche flourished. The beautiful girl's happiness lasted all her life, which was long; her story, along with Alix's, proves the idea that I earlier proposed, that often

> Gentle and courtly language
> Is better than any rich accoutrement.

I do not know, Madame, what you think of this tale, but it seems to me no more incredible than many of the stories recounted in ancient Greece, and I would just as soon say that pearls and rubies came from Blanche's mouth to express the effects of eloquence as I would say that lightning bolts burst from the mouth of Pericles. Story for story, it seems to me that those of ancient Gaul are just as good as those of the Greeks. And fairies have just as much right to work wonders as the gods of the fables.

I will let you ponder that question for yourself, though for my part I have no doubts. What I do fear is that those who hear these tales, and who know of your fine talents, might conceive the idea that it is by means of some fairy magic that you speak so pleasingly and so truly. That would be an entirely plausible idea, yes, for finding in you such wisdom and eloquence, it is difficult not to conclude that there is some enchantment involved.

---

19. An allusion to the phrase "au coin d'un bois," from Perrault's tale "Les fées" ("The Fairies"; 253).

Nonetheless, you must be given credit; and so I, who know firsthand the true nature of your charms, hereby announce in all sincerity that there is no *fairy gift* at work in you, but only the *gift of the heavens*, which, thus favoring you, have made you *Eloquentia Nativa* in the flesh.

HENRIETTE-JULIE DE CASTELNAU, COMTESSE DE MURAT

(1668?–1716)

Little is known about Henriette-Julie de Castelnau's childhood. The author was born into a prominent aristocratic family and married Nicolas de Murat, an alliance that bestowed upon her the title of comtesse. She became active as a writer in the early 1690s, but her life and reputation soon became so tainted by scandal that it is now difficult to filter fact from rumor. Many scholars have suggested that Murat published a pamphlet in 1694 that was seen as libelous against the court and resulted in her exile from Paris. Other evidence suggests that Murat must have written her 1690s works—including the *contes*—from Paris. Other *conteuses* dedicated their tales to her, such as Marie-Jeanne L'héritier de Villandon's "L'adroite princesse" (1696; see "The Quick-Witted Princess," included in this volume). Murat was said to frequent the literary salons of Anne-Thérèse de Marguenat de Courcelles, marquise de Lambert, in Paris. In the "Avertissement," or preface, to her *Histoires sublimes et allégoriques* (*Sublime and Allegorical Stories*), Murat writes that everybody, including herself, was borrowing stories from the Italian writer Giovan Francesco Straparola (see also Bottigheimer 23). Thus, the conversations in which Murat was participating were consistent with those circulating in Paris.

Her first two volumes of *contes* were published in 1698: *Contes de fées* (*Fairy Tales*) and *Les nouveaux contes de fées* (*New Fairy Tales*). *Histoires sublimes et allégoriques* followed in 1699. The period

of her life beginning in 1700 is scattered with more scandalous accusations and banishment from the court. Known as a
"woman of little virtue" and imprisoned for her lesbianism, Murat was confined in the castle of Loches, then, after an escape
attempt in 1706, in the castle prison of Saumur, then in the
castle of Angers, before being returned again to Loches.
When her freedom was finally restored by the Duke d'Orléans
after Louis XIV's death in 1715, Murat was suffering from ill
health. She withdrew to her grandmother's castle in what is
today the French department of Maine and died there in
September 1716.

Like many of the other *conteuses*, Murat was fond of com-
bining French lore with characters and themes from Greco-
Roman mythology; yet she went on to develop original plot-
lines. In her first volume of tales, Murat writes that she can
offer "quelques Contes de ma façon" ("several tales in [her]
own manner") and dedicates the volume to "Fées modernes"
("modern fairies"; *Contes* 200, 199). Her tales include lengthy
descriptions that often feel as though they would be more at
home in a novella or short novel. In questions of love, Murat's
contes are among the most dystopian of the volume, which is
why we have chosen to place them at the end. Unhappy endings, unhappy relationships, and the failure of magic to solve
problems when love is in play are omnipresent themes in Murat's tales.

Further Reading

Bottigheimer, Ruth. "France's First Fairy Tales: The Restoration and Rise Narratives of *Les facetieuses nuitz du Seigneur
François Straparole*." *Marvels and Tales*, vol. 19, no. 1, 2005,
pp. 17–31.

Cromer, Sylvie. "'Le sauvage': Histoire sublime et allégorique
de Madame de Murat." *Marvels and Tales*, vol. 1, no. 1, 1987,
pp. 2–19.

Murat, Henriette-Julie de Castelnau, comtesse de. "Avertisse-ment." *Histoires sublimes et allégoriques,* Florentin et Pierre Delaulne, 1699.

———. *Contes.* Edited by Geneviève Patard, Champion, 2006. Bibliothèque des génies et des fées 3.

Patard, Geneviève. "Henriette-Julie de Castelnau, Countess de Murat (1668?–1716)." Translated and adapted by Sophie Raynard. *The Teller's Tale: Lives of the Classic Fairy-Tale Writers,* edited by Sophie Raynard, State U of New York P, 2013, pp. 81–89.

Robinson, David M. "The Abominable Madame de Murat." *Homosexuality in French History and Culture,* edited by Jeffrey Merrick and Michael Sibalis, Harrington Park Press, 2001, pp. 53–67.

Welch, Marcelle Maistre. "Manipulation du discours féerique dans les *Contes de fées* de Mme de Murat." *Cahiers du dix-septième,* vol. 5, no. 1, 1991, pp. 21–29.

The Pleasant Punishment

Once there was a great king who fell desperately in love with a beautiful princess of his court. He told her of his feelings as soon as he began to feel them himself, for kings have privileges that ordinary lovers are denied. The princess was in no way offended, knowing that his love might well lead her to a place on the throne, but for the king's sake she took care to seem as demure and respectable as she was charming. He married her, and the wedding was a ceremony of extraordinary opulence; more extraordinary still, he became a husband without ceasing to be a lover. The pleasures of their tender union were troubled only by the regret that they had no children to perpetuate their happiness and their kingdom.

Hungry for the consolation of hope if nothing more, the king resolved to consult a fairy he believed he could count among his friends. Her name was Formidable, but she had

not proven so for the king.[1] They say that the annals of
that land are still full of scandalous songs about her, for
poets have always been brave souls. They had to be, since
the fairy was greatly respected and seemed so untamable
that it was nearly impossible to imagine her captured by
the power of love—but was there ever a heart that could
escape it? The king was a keen-eyed and worldly man; he
knew full well that appearances are often deceptive.[2] He
had first met Formidable in a wood where he was hunting,
and he had found her person so comely, and her manner
so delightful, that the he did not doubt for a moment she
was trying to attract him. Rarely are such charms displayed without some motive behind them. The king fell in
love with her, and his fairy found it was more pleasant to
be loved than to be feared. Their romance went on for
some years, but one day Formidable, who had come to see
her lover's heart as hers in perpetuity, allowed the king to
glimpse her in her true form. She was no longer young,
she was far from beautiful; seeing the look on the king's

---

1. By a strange quirk of language, the French word *formidable* used to
mean precisely what the English word *formidable* currently means:
fearsome, daunting. (In modern French parlance, *formidable* is more
likely to mean "wonderful" or "fantastic.") The word comes from the
Latin *formidare*: to dread or fear.

2. The seventeenth century was a time during which elite society
insisted on the importance of *vraisemblance* (having the appearance of
truth) in art, such that, despite a consciousness that things may not always be what they seem, there remained an insistence that people,
texts, and events conform to the *vraisemblable*.

face, she bitterly regretted her naive faith in herself, and she soon came to understand that even the tenderest sentiments cannot touch another's heart or satisfy love's demands if they are not supported by a pretty face. The king was ashamed: he had fallen in love with nothing more than a beautiful idea.

From that moment on, he no longer loved the fairy; he respected and admired her, but that was all. Formidable was a proud woman, and pretended she was perfectly happy to have nothing more than the king's friendship; indeed, she put on so fine an act that that she convinced him he had no better friend. She even attended his wedding, along with all the other fairies of the land, lest a spiteful refusal let it be thought she had some reason to be distressed at the marriage.

And so, counting on his former mistress's friendship, the king set off to pay her a visit. Formidable lived in a palace of flame-colored marble surrounded by a vast forest, at the end of prodigiously long avenue guarded on either side by a hundred lions, also the color of flame: she had enchanted all the creatures of her forest, and had turned them all her favorite color. The avenue led to a great square courtyard, where a magnificently armed troop of Moors,[3] dressed in flame and gold, stood on

---

3. A Moor is "a member of a people of mixed Arab and Berber ancestry inhabiting ancient Mauretania in North Africa and conquering Spain in the 8th century A.D." ("Moor"). By the time of these tales (in what we

perpetual watch. The king crossed the forest alone, knowing the way perfectly, and walked without danger along the avenue, having first tossed the lions a handful of buttercups the fairy had given him long before to ensure his safe passage; no sooner had the king thrown out those sweet flowers than the lions turned docile and harmless. Then he came to the Moorish guards; at first they trained their arrows on him, but the king strew them with pomegranate flowers given him by the fairy along with the buttercups, and the Moors simply fired into the air, then lined up in two ranks and stood at attention to let him pass by.

He entered Formidable's palace and found her in a salon, sitting on a ruby throne, surrounded by twelve Moorish maidservants dressed in gold and flame-colored muslin. Her dress was like theirs, but was so covered with precious stones that she shone like the sun; she was only the more beautiful for it. The king stood still for a moment before entering the room, discreetly watching and listening. He saw a pile of books on a red marble table at the fairy's side; he saw her pick one up as she continued her lesson, for she was instructing the Moorish women in the secrets that make fairies so powerful—but

---

might today consider a textbook example of Orientalism), Moorish culture had become synonymous in France with splendor and elegance; no doubt for that reason, the fairies of these stories habitually surround themselves with Moorish servants, guards, and so on.

only those secrets that ruin the contentment and tranquility of men. She took great care to teach them nothing that might bring a man happiness. Seeing this, the king conceived a deep hatred for the fairy. He burst in, interrupting that dreadful lesson and catching Formidable off guard, but she quickly recovered her poise and even dismissed her servants. She glared superciliously at the king. "What are you doing here, faithless prince?" she asked. "Why do you once again allow your odious presence to trouble the rest I seek to enjoy here?" Not expecting that answer, the king was struck dumb with surprise. The fairy opened one of her books and went on, "I can see perfectly well what you want; yes, you will have a daughter with that princess you so unjustly chose over me, but do not be so foolish as to believe you will be happy forever, for the time of my vengeance has come. Your daughter will be hated by all, just as much as I once tenderly loved you." The king tried desperately to calm the fairy's anger, but to no avail: love had given way to hate, and only love could soothe the fairy, pity and generosity being sentiments she knew nothing of. She proudly ordered the king out of her palace, throwing open the door to an aviary and releasing a flame-colored· parrot. "Follow this bird," she said to him, "and be grateful for my clemency, which will protect you from the fury of my lions and my guards." The bird flew off, the king followed, and by a route unknown to him, far shorter than the one he'd taken to come, he was led back to his kingdom.

On his return, the queen found him downcast, and so insistently asked him why that in the end he told her of the fairy's cruel prediction, though he said nothing of what had once happened between them, to avoid burdening the beautiful queen with yet another sorrow. She knew that a fairy cannot entirely prevent what another fairy has foreseen, but she can nevertheless ease its pains. "I must go and see Lumineuse, the sovereign of the Empire Heureux,"[4] she said. "Lumineuse is a celebrated fairy who likes nothing more than to aid the afflicted. She's a relative of mine, and has always favored me—she even predicted the happy fate that love would bring me." The king strongly approved of the queen's voyage, and he had high hopes of its success. Once her coach and her escort were ready, she set off to find Lumineuse, who bore that name because her beauty shone so brightly that it could scarcely be looked on, and the goodness of her soul perfectly mirrored her beauty.

The queen came to a vast open plain, and from afar spied a tall tower; it stood in plain sight, but she would have to make many detours before she reached it. The tower was made of white marble; it had no door, and its arched windows were pure crystal. A fine river whose

---

4. That is, the Happy Empire, or the Empire of Happiness.

rippling surface shone like silver lapped at its base, after having circled it nine times. The queen and her court came to the river's edge where it began its first loop around the fairy's abode. The queen crossed it on a bridge of white poppies, made as sound and sturdy as bronze by Lumineuse's power. Even made of flowers, it was a redoubtable bridge: it had the power to cast anyone who crossed it against the fairy's will into a seven-year sleep. Just past the bridge, the queen spied half a dozen magnificently attired young men, sleeping on grass beds under leafy pavilions. These were princes who had fallen in love with the fairy; since Lumineuse did not want to hear one word about love, she had not allowed them to come further. With the bridge behind her, the queen found herself in the first meadow between the bends of the river; it was occupied by a charming labyrinth, all of jasmine and oleander, everything as white as can be, for that was the color Lumineuse loved best. After she had admired that beautiful promenade, and easily found her way through its many twists and turns—which defeated only those good Lumineuse did not want to see—the queen crossed the river a second time, on a bridge of white windflowers. Here the river made its second turn, and the expanse of land before the third loop was taken up by a forest of ever-blooming acacias, traversed by pathways so delightfully shaded that the sun could not hope to get through to them. In those trees perched gentle doves whose feathers brought shame to snow, as well as a multitude of white canaries singing in delightful concert. With one stroke of her wand, Lumineuse had taught them all the prettiest and most pleasing songs in the world.

At the end of that splendid forest lay a bridge made of tuberoses, which led to a lovely grove of trees so heavy with beautiful, delicious fruit that even the smallest of them far outshone the Garden of the Hesperides.[5] Every evening she spent in that orchard, the queen found it arrayed with the finest tents in the world, which she entered to find a magnificent repast just laid out without even one of her skillful, diligent servants in sight. The fairy had seen in her books that the queen would be coming, and wanted to give her a comfortable journey; she did not wish the queen to suffer even a moment of weariness. To leave that beautiful spot, the queen crossed the river on a bridge of white carnations and entered the fairy's park. It was as beautiful as all that had come before; sometimes the fairy came there to hunt, for it was filled with an incalculable number of white does and stags, as well as other beasts of the same color. White greyhounds lay on the grass here and there, alongside

---

5. In Greek mythology, the Hesperides are three sisters, the daughters of Hesperus (who is the son of the dawn goddess Eos and who often personifies the evening star). The garden of the Hesperides is famous for its golden apple tree guarded by a dragon.

white does, white rabbits, and other usually wild beasts who were not wild there. By her art, the fairy had tamed them, and when the dogs chased after some creature to amuse Lumineuse, they seemed to understand that it was only a game, for they did everything they should do in such circumstances, except that they never caused pain. Here the river made its fifth loop around the fairy's home.

To leave this park, the queen crossed a bridge of little jasmine flowers and found herself in a charming hamlet. All the little houses were built of alabaster; the inhabitants of that adorable place were the fairy's subjects. They watched over her flock, dressed in silver muslin, crowned with garlands of flowers, their crooks shining with precious gems. All the sheep were dazzlingly white, all the shepherdesses young and beautiful, and Lumineuse was too fond of the color white to have neglected to give them a complexion so fair that the very sun seemed to make it grow lighter. All the shepherds were handsome, and the one thing for which this agreeable land could be faulted for was that there was not one dark-haired beauty to be seen. The shepherdesses greeted the queen, presenting her with porcelain vases filled with all the world's most perfect flowers. Like her court, the queen was charmed by the refinement she found everywhere on her journey, and believed it boded well for the favor she intended to ask of the fairy.

As she set off to leave the hamlet, a young shepherdess came toward the queen with a little greyhound on a white velvet cushion embroidered with silver and pearls; the greyhound could scarcely be made out against its pillow, so similar were their colors. "The fairy Lumineuse, sovereign of the Empire Heureux," said the young shepherdess to the queen, "has asked me to present you with Blanc-Blanc, for such is this little greyhound's name; she has the honor of being loved by Lumineuse, whose art has made Blanc-Blanc a prodigy of nature, and she has commanded her to lead you to her tower. Great princess, you need only turn her loose and follow after her."

The queen took the little greyhound with pleasure, charmed by the fairy's thoughtfulness. She caressed Blanc-Blanc, who returned her affection with lucidity and elegance; with that the dog gracefully leapt to the ground and began to walk ahead of the queen as all the court followed after. They came to the river, which here made its sixth turn, and were astonished to find no bridge by which to cross it. The fairy did not want her shepherds disturbing her in her retreat, and so there was no bridge at that spot, except when she wanted to visit the hamlet or receive her friends there. The queen was pondering this matter when she heard Blanc-Blanc bark three times; all at once a zephyr shook the trees on the other side of the river, showering such a blizzard of orange-tree flowers onto the water that they formed a bridge for the queen. She expressed her thanks to Blanc-Blanc with caresses, and soon found herself in an avenue of delightful myrtle and orange trees; walking to the end without weariness despite its great length, she arrived once again at the bank of the river, now making its seventh turn. She saw no bridge, but the memory of that morning's adventure reassured her. Blanc-Blanc stamped three times with her little paw, and a bridge of white hyacinths appeared. Crossing that bridge, the queen entered a meadow carpeted with flowers; in the middle stood her beautiful tents, and she rested there before going on, soon finding herself once again at the water's edge. There was no way across, but Blanc-Blanc stepped forward to drink from that beautiful river, and at once a bridge of white roses appeared. The queen crossed that bridge and entered the fairy's garden, so full of marvelous flowers, extraordinary fountains, and breathtaking statues that no words would do it justice. Were the queen not so terribly impatient to prevent the sorrows promised her by the cruel Formidable, she would gladly have lingered there for some time. Her entire court was sorry to leave that glorious garden, but they had no choice but to follow Blanc-Blanc as she led the queen to the river's last loop around Lumineuse's tower. At long last, the queen could see that tower from close up, with only the river between them: she gazed at it with pleasure, for it marked the final destination of her journey. On the wall of that tower she read this inscription, etched in letters of gold:

Here is the charming abode
Of perfect and unbroken happiness;
Lumineuse built this beautiful place,
Where joy is allowed and love banished,
Though she seems made for nothing else.

The inscription had been placed there in Lumineuse's honor by the most renowned fairies of her time, wanting posterity to have some record of their friendship and esteem. As the queen waited happily by the river, Blanc-Blanc swam to the opposite bank, plunged underwater like a bird, and reappeared with a mother-of-pearl shell; she then dropped that shell back into the river. Hearing that sound, six beautiful nymphs dressed in gleaming sheaths threw open a huge crystal window, and out came a pearl staircase that slowly descended toward the queen. Blanc-Blanc briskly climbed to the fairy's window and went in. The queen followed by the same route, but the steps vanished behind her as she climbed, preventing anyone from doing as she did. She entered Lumineuse's beautiful tower, and the sylphs closed the window a moment after.

The queen's courtiers were frantic to see her disappear with no way to follow her, for they loved her deeply. Their wails could be heard even in the room where Lumineuse was welcoming the queen; to ease their torment, the fairy dispatched a nymph to guide them to a hamlet where they could await her return. Their hope was reborn the moment they saw the pearl staircase re-appear; the nymph came down to them, and the queen came to the window to bid them follow her and do as she said. She herself stayed behind with the fairy who had welcomed her with such great opulence and with a divine demeanor that never failed to melt any heart. The queen remained with her for three days, not time enough to see all the marvels of Lumineuse's tower: it would have taken centuries to admire each one as it deserved, to say nothing of the fairy's beauty. On the fourth day, after she had lavished the queen with presents as sumptuous as they were delightful, Lumineuse said to her, "Beautiful queen, I am sorry that I cannot undo the sorrows with which Formidable has threatened you, but that is the doing of fate, which allows us to give generously to those we favor but forbids us to ward off any misery another fairy has ordained. Thus, to console you for the unhappiness that awaits you, I promise that before this year is over you will have a daughter so beautiful that everyone who lays eyes on her will be charmed—and," the fairy added, "I will also bring about the birth of a prince who will be worthy of her." Thanks to that happy prediction, the queen could for the moment forget Formidable's hatred and all the sorrow that lay ahead.

Lumineuse did not say how Formidable came to be her enemy. Even quarreling fairies take pains to protect each other's secrets if those secrets might diminish them in the eyes of mortals; it is said that they are the only women on earth with the generosity of spirit never to speak ill of each other.

Once the queen had poured out her thanks, Lumineuse ordered twelve of her nymphs to pick up twelve loads of gifts and accompany the queen to the hamlet. Lumineuse herself preceded her on the pearl staircase that appeared the moment she opened the window. At the bottom of the steps, the queen and the nymphs found a silver carriage pulled by six white does with diamond-studded harnesses; in the coachman's seat sat a child as beautiful as a flower. The nymphs followed the carriage on white horses whose beauty rivaled the steeds that pull the sun's winged chariot. The queen was thus elegantly conveyed to the hamlet, where she found her overjoyed courtiers; the nymphs soon took their leave, but only after presenting the queen with their twelve magnificent horses—graced by the fairy with the gift of never tiring—and passing on Lumineuse's wish that they be given to the king on her behalf.

Marveling at the fairy's generosity, the queen returned to her realm. The king came to meet her at the border, and was so delighted at her return and the good news she had brought from Lumineuse that he called for a day of public rejoicing; word of that celebration reached Formidable, redoubling her fury and her hatred of the king. The queen found herself pregnant soon after her homecoming, and she was sure the child-to-be was the beautiful princess who would charm every heart, for Lumineuse had promised the child would be born by year's end. Meanwhile, Formidable had not said when she would wreak her vengeance, but surely she would not put it off for long. The queen gave birth to two princesses; from the eagerness she immediately felt to kiss the firstborn, she knew which was the one promised by Lumineuse.

For that child lived up to the fairy's promises in every way; no creature in the world was so beautiful. The king and the midwives gathered around to admire her, completely ignoring her sister; but the queen, sensing from their neglect that Formidable's prediction had been borne out at the same time as Lumineuse's, ordered more than once that the second child be seen to every bit as attentively as the first.

The midwives obeyed her with a reticence they could not quite overcome, one that the king and queen could scarcely condemn, for they felt it themselves. Lumineuse swiftly came riding in on a cloud and dubbed the beautiful princess Aimée, wanting to give her a name that suited the destiny she had promised her. The king greeted Lumineuse with all the respect she deserved; she promised the queen that she would always watch over Aimée, and gave her no further gifts, for she had already endowed her with everything. As for the other princess, in vain did the king give her the name of one of his provinces: little by little, they all took to calling her Naimée, in cruel contrast with her sister.[6]

When the princesses turned twelve, Formidable demanded that they be removed from the court, to lessen the hatred endured by the one, she said, and the love enjoyed by the other. Lumineuse allowed Formidable to issue this command, sure that nothing could stop beautiful Aimée from reigning in her father's kingdom and in every heart. She had bestowed on her so many graces that one glimpse of the child silenced all doubt of that. Hoping to quell the relentless hatred with which Formidable was besieging his household, the king made up his mind to obey her. He sent the two princesses, along with an escort of young, good-hearted courtiers, to a marvelous chateau of his, at the very edge of his kingdom: he called it the Chateau des Portraits. It was a place in every way worthy of the ingenious fairy who had built it four thousand years before: the gardens and surrounding promenades were splendid, but finest of all was a gallery that stretched on and on as far as the eye could see, its walls lined with the portraits of all the princes and princesses of royal blood from that kingdom and its neighbors. Once they

---

6. *Aimée* would of course mean "loved" or "beloved"; *Naimée* does not literally mean "unloved" but unambiguously implies that negation.

turned fifteen their portraits abruptly appeared on the wall, painted with a skill that any mere mortal artist could imitate feebly at best. That gift would go on being given until the day the most beautiful princess in the world found her way into the chateau.

The gallery lay between two vast, magnificent apartments, which were occupied by the two princesses. They had the same teachers, the same education; the charming Aimée was taught nothing that was not also taught to her sister. But Formidable regularly visited to give Naimée lessons that corrupted everything she had learned, just as Lumineuse came to make Aimée worthy of the whole universe's admiration through her good counsel. The princesses and their court had lived in that isolated chateau for three years when one day they heard a strange sound, followed by the most charming music. Everyone looked all around to discern the source of that noise and that pleasant melody; finally they spied three portraits in three previously empty niches.

The first was crowned with flowers by two Cupids, one gazing on that beautiful face with all the attention it deserved, seeming to forget all about the arrow he was about to shoot from his bow, the other holding a little ribbon on which were written these lines:

On Aimée's birth wise nature gave her
Every earthly beauty, which will never fade;

> The Graces worked to perfect her charms,
> And Venus gave her her belt, to keep forever.[7]

But there was no need for those words to show that this was the portrait of the lovely Aimée, for the painting depicted her every feature, along with the charming grace that drew every heart to her. Her skin was dazzlingly fair, her cheeks flushed with the most beautiful pink. Her face was round, her hair breathtakingly blond, her eyes blue but so bright that everyone who had the pleasure of seeing them found there was no need for Lumineuse to have endowed Aimée with a gift that she already owned. Her mouth was charming, her teeth as white as her skin, and her smile seemed to have been lent to her by Venus herself.

Such was the divine portrait that occupied one end of the gallery. The other depicted Naimée: blond, not without beauty, but exactly like her, the portrait was unpleasant to look at. These words were written above it, in letters of gold:

> With all the beauty in her face
> In no heart will Naimée find a place;
> Let this be a lesson for all the ages to come:
> Beauty is nothing without wit and grace.

---

7. Venus was the Roman name of Aphrodite, the Greek goddess of love, beauty, sexual desire, and fertility, who was well-known for her golden belt. When she wore it, she was particularly irresistible; she sometimes bestowed it upon others as a sign of her favor.

The two princesses and their court stood lost in contemplation of those two portraits. When Aimee, who had no vanity concerning her own charms, and who left the task of admiring them to the rest of the world, cast her eyes on the third portrait that had appeared along with the other two, she found in it something worthy of her attention: it showed a young prince, a thousand times more beautiful than Eros himself. He seemed more a god than a man, with black hair falling in thick curls over his shoulders, and his eyes gave promise of a mind as lively as his person was appealing. Below the portrait were written these words:

The Prince of the Île Galante.

His beauty left the entire crowd speechless, but no one was more moved than the beautiful Aimée! An unfamiliar emotion stirred her young heart; even Naimée, at the sight of that glorious portrait, was gripped by a passion that no one would ever feel for her. No one was surprised by this strange happening, for marvels were commonplace in that chateau. The king and the queen came to call on the princesses; they had many copies made of their portraits, and sent them out to all the neighboring kingdoms.[8] But whenever Aimée was alone,

---

8. Portrait halls, often filled with magical portraits with the powers to move or talk, are common features of these fairy tales. In real life, portraits were often copied and circulated to potential suitors and were thus an important economic and social currency. For another

she gave in to an uncontrollable urge and returned to the gallery, her every thought and gaze fixed on the prince of the Île Galante, who seemed worthy of both.

Naimée, who had nothing in common with her sister save that attraction to the prince's portrait, also found her way into the gallery nearly every day. Her burgeoning passion so deepened her hatred of the beautiful princess that, unable to discover the secret to hurting her, she tirelessly begged Formidable to avenge her of her sister's charms. That wicked fairy never refused an opportunity for mischief; and so, following her own inclination and Naimée's entreaties, she went looking for the lovely princess as she strolled on the banks of a river that flowed past the Chateau des Portraits. "Go now," Formidable said to her, touching her with an ebony wand. "Go, and follow this riverbank forever, until you have found someone who hates you as much as I; until that day you will have no home in the world of men." Hearing those terrible words, the princess began to weep. What tears! In all the universe, only Formidable's heart was unmoved by them.

Lumineuse came running to console poor Aimée. "Do not be afraid," she said, "for the voyage Formidable has just condemned you to will end in a pleasant adventure, and

example in this volume, see Marie-Jeanne L'héritier's "The Quick-Witted Princess."

until that day you will encounter only delights." Hearing these promising words, Aimée went on her way; her only regret was that she would never again lay her eyes on the prince of the Île Galante's portrait but she did not dare reveal that sorrow to the fairy. As she walked on, she found that everything around her seemed keenly sensitive to her charms. Wherever she went, only the mild west wind blew. Everywhere she found nymphs eager to serve her with great respect. Carpets of flowers bloomed in the fields as she drew near, and when the sun was too hot, the woods took care to deepen the shadows they cast. And so the beautiful princess continued her delightful wanderings. But Lumineuse did not limit her vengeance to taking the sting out of Formidable's plan; she went and found Naimée, then tapped her with an ivory wand and said, "Go now, go and follow the riverbank, never to rest until you have found someone who loves you as much as you deserve to be unloved." Off Naimée went, and no one missed her.

Even Formidable, who was perfectly happy as long as she was torturing someone, thought no more of Naimée, and did not bother to protect her. And so the two princesses journeyed on, Naimée with every conceivable weariness, the finest flowers changing to thorns as she approached, and the beautiful princess with all the pleasures that Lumineuse had led her to expect, and some even sweeter than she had been promised.

Just as a beautiful day was coming to a close, at the hour the sun goes to rest in the arms of Thetis,[9] Aimée sat down on the riverbank, and a multitude of flowers sprang up around her, making a sort of parterre whose charms she would have gazed on longer had she not glimpsed on the river an object that immediately robbed her of all other thoughts: a little boat of amethyst, ornamented with a thousand banderoles of the same color, bearing courtly ciphers and devices.[10] Twelve young men dressed in light clothes of linen gray and silver, crowned with garlands of immortelles, were rowing that boat so diligently that a moment later it was close by the riverbank, allowing beautiful Aimée to observe it in all its beauty. It was with a very pleasant astonishment that she saw her name and ciphers everywhere: a moment later, the princess recognized her own portrait on a little topaz altar that stood in the middle of the boat, and beneath it these words:

If this be not Love, then what might Love be?

Her first impulse was to cry out in enchantment; but then she found herself afraid at the thought of these strangers coming ashore, however gentlemanly they seemed. "Everything I see here tells me I am loved by a

---

9. Thetis: in Greek mythology, one of the goddesses of the sea, and mother of Achilles.

10. A cipher is generally a sort of stylized monogram; a device is a little allegorical image.

man I do not know," Aimée told herself, "but I believe no one but the prince of the Île Galante could be worthy of making me feel the emotions this man seems to feel. O fateful portrait!" she added. "Why did destiny offer you to my eyes at an age when I was so perfectly defenseless, before I had even learned that one could love something more tenderly than flowers?"

That thought was followed by several melancholy sighs; she would have remained in that quiet reverie for some time had she not been roused by a delightful concert of musical instruments. She looked toward the boat, whence these pleasing sounds were coming. A man whose face she could not see, dressed in a magnificent garment of the same color that shone on all his crew, seemed to be staring transfixed at her portrait as six beautiful nymphs played in charming harmony, accompanying him as he sang these words, all the while gazing on the princess's beautiful portrait. The air was by Du Boulay:[11]

> Let everything speak of my love,
> And the charms of my beloved,
> For Aimée has more delights than Love itself;

---

11. Du Boulay: In the Champion edition, Geneviève Patard identifies this author as Michel du Boulay, a seventeenth-century librettist. Notably, he composed *Zéphire et Flore* (1688) and *Orphée* (1690), tragedies that were put to music by Louis and Jean-Louis Lully (Murat, "L'heureuse peine" 193). In the original text, Murat spells his name *Duboulai*.

O Nymphs, echo my deep emotion

And say again one by one

That everything speaks of my love,

And the charms of my beloved.

The Graces abandon the heavens to follow her,

Leaving the Queen of Cythera[12] without regret;

The pleasure of seeing her, the sweetness of
  pleasing her,

Is better than the home and the pleasure
  of the Gods.

Aimée has more delights than love itself;

O Nymphs, echo my deep emotion,

And say again one by one

That everything speaks of my love,

And the charms of my beloved.

One glance from her and a heart is on fire;

Everything bows down to her, everything
  surrenders,

And until the happy time when her charms first lit
  up this world

No one must ever have loved.

---

12. The Greek island of Cythera—today Kythira—was one legendary home of Aphrodite. In eighteenth-century France, "to go to Cythera" meant to give oneself up to the pleasures of love; see Jean-Antoine Watteau's painting *L'embarquement pour Cythère* (*Pilgrimage to Cythera*).

Aimée has more delights than love itself,

O Nymphs, echo my deep emotion,

And say again one by one

That everything speaks of my love,

And the charms of my beloved.

The harmonies of this concert kept the beautiful Aimée standing in delight on the riverbank; once it was done, the stranger turned his head and allowed her to glimpse, with as much shock as pleasure, the glorious features of the prince of the Île Galante. What a surprise! What a joy to see before her that charming prince, and to learn that his thoughts were filled with her alone! Only one who knows how to love perfectly as they did in the days of the fairies could possibly understand what the young princess was then feeling.

The prince of the Île Galante felt the same surprise. He hurried to disembark on the blessed riverbank that had offered the divine Aimée to his gaze. She could not bring herself to flee so perfect a prince, and a thousand times she accused fate of her weakness: in such moments as this, no one ever fails to pin the blame on fate. There are no words to express what the young lovers said to each other, and indeed often they made their meaning clear without words. It was Lumineuse who had led that beautiful boat and Aimée's steps to this place; all at once she appeared, reassuring the timid princess just when she had resolved to tear herself away from that charming, dangerous prince. She informed them that they were destined to love each other and to come together for all time. "But," added the fairy, "before that happy day, you must complete the journey Formidable has ordained."

A fairy is not to be disobeyed: the beautiful Aimée and the prince were so happy to be together that anything that kept them at each other's side seemed the sweetest thing they could wish for. And so they continued their journey, sometimes in the pretty boat, sometimes crossing through a beautiful, empty expanse irrigated by the river. It was in that quiet spot that the prince of the Île Galante lost the last vestige of tranquility that remained in his heart. He told the beautiful princess of everything he had felt for her since the happy day when her divine portrait had arrived at his court. One day, he recounted, he had been walking by the water and dreaming of his love when Lumineuse appeared and showed him the amethyst boat, ordering him to climb aboard, promising that his journey and his love would come to a happy end. As the prince and the beautiful Aimée approached the end of the journey imposed on them by Formidable, their ardor grew with each passing day, and they were both so happy that they dreaded the day when their travels would be done, not wanting to occupy their minds with anything but their own tender feelings. And all the while Naimée too was coming to the end of her wretched journey.

Little by little the river's course brought the two princesses to the Île Galante, and they arrived at the same time. Lumineuse did not fail to join them. She told Aimée that Formidable's vengeance was now satisfied, since by meeting her sister she was finding the one person in the world who could possibly hate her. "And so Naimée's voyage is done as well," said the beautiful princess, "for nothing ever diminished the friendship I feel for her." She then implored the fairy to soften her sister's sad fate if she could, but that favor sought on Naimée's behalf came to nothing: the moment she saw the prince of the Île Galante, recognizing him as the man whose portrait had so touched her heart, and heard Lumineuse say that the time for his marriage with young Aimée was approaching, Naimée threw herself into the river. She had followed the course of that river for a year, and despite her unhappiness she had never sought the final recourse of death—but the sorrows of love sting far more bitterly than those of fortune.

Seeing the princess drop into the water, Lumineuse changed her into a little creature that to this day expresses poor Naimée's mood by its strange way of walking.[13] Her fate went on unchanged even after her death, for she was not missed. Aimée shed a few tears, but what

---

13. According to at least one critic, the creature in question is a crayfish. There is in fact nothing strange about the way crayfish walk, but they do swim backward abruptly when confronted with danger—

sorrow could not be consoled by the prince of the Île Galante! She was so moved by his affection that she was almost unmoved by the many festivities invented to welcome her to his kingdom; the prince too scarcely took part in them. When one is truly in love, the only pleasure one can know is the pleasure of being loved by one's beloved.

Told of these events by Lumineuse, the king and the queen came to join their beloved daughter. It was in their presence that the good-hearted fairy announced that fair Aimée had had the glory of putting an end to the adventure of the Chateau des Portraits, for nothing so beautiful had yet appeared in all the world. The love of the prince of the Île Galante was too intense to wait any longer: he begged the queen and king to consent to his happiness, and Lumineuse herself graced that beautiful, long-desired day with her presence. The wedding was held with all the magnificence that might be expected of fairies and kings, but however happy that day might have been, I shall not seek to describe it, for no matter what happy love promises itself, a wedding is almost always a sad celebration.

> So long as Love wreaks its fears and torments,
> And the sweet intoxications it inspires,

---

hence the curiously widespread belief that they walk backward or sideways.

There remain a hundred things to say

For poets and for lovers.

But when the wedding comes, in vain do

> we invoke

The god of poetry and the nine eloquent sisters:[14]

For it is the fate of all love, and of every author

To fail with the epithalamium.[15]

---

14. The nine muses in Greek mythology.

15. An epithalamium is a poem written to be declaimed as a newly wedded couple make their way to their room for the wedding night. Note Murat's delightful cynicism (which might remind us of the last lines of "Tufty Riquet"): just as no poet can manage to write an epithalamium worthy of the moment, love does not live long after the epithalamium has been read.

ANGUILLETTE

However glorious the station to which fate lifts its favorites, no happiness is without its travails. No one who knows anything about fairies can fail to know that for all their wisdom they have never freed themselves of the inconvenience of changing form for a few days each month, turning into some animal of the land, the air, or the waters. Those are dangerous days, for the fairies become easy targets for the violent ways of mankind; often it is only with great difficulty that they preserve themselves against the perils that come with that cruel obligation.

One such fairy, whose habit was to change into an eel, had the misfortune one day of being caught by fishermen. They carried her away through a pleasant meadow to a little basin, a way station for fish bound for the king's dinner table. Anguillette, as the fairy was named,[1] found herself surrounded by a crowd of beautiful fish fated like

---

1. That is, "little eel."

her to live only a few hours more: she had heard the fishermen discussing the feast that would take place that very evening, for which these succulent fish had been specifically chosen. What a thing for the poor fairy to hear! A thousand times she lamented her fate, sighing in grief, hiding away deep in the water to mourn in peace; but all at once she found in her an indomitable will to flee the threat that hung over her, and she began to search for some way out of the reservoir and back to the nearby river. But in vain: the basin was too deep, and she could not escape it unaided. And now, to compound her woe, she saw the fishermen coming near. They cast their nets over the water; Anguillette did her best to dodge them, and did so handily, though she knew she could only delay her demise for a few moments more.

The king's youngest daughter had come out for a walk in the meadow, and she stopped by the basin to watch the fishing. The rays of the setting sun lit the waters, making Anguillette's skin shine out brightly among the many colors around her. Thinking this a most beautiful sight, the young princess ordered the men to catch that fish and give it to her. They obeyed, and so the poor fairy found herself held between two hands that would decide if she lived or died.

The princess gazed on Anguillette for a few moments, and then felt a sudden surge of pity; she ran straight off to the riverbank to put her back in the water.

This unexpected good turn filled the fairy's heart with gratitude. She came to the surface again and said to the princess, "I owe you my life, good Plousine" (for that was her name), "but this is a lucky day for you too." Seeing the princess about to run away, she went on, "Don't be afraid; I am a fairy, and I will prove it by a multitude of favors I will do you."

No one was shocked to see a fairy in those days; Plousine's fear thus quickly vanished, and she listened closely to Anguillette's pleasing promises. She was just beginning to answer her when the fairy interrupted, "Do not thank me now; wait until you have received my gifts. Go now, young princess, and come back to this spot tomorrow morning; consider the wish you would like to make, and I will grant it immediately. Choose between perfect beauty, a fine mind, or untold riches." With these words, Anguillette dove into the depths, leaving Plousine very pleased with this turn of events.

She resolved to tell no one what had happened, "for," she mused, "if it turns out that Anguillette has deceived me, then my sisters will believe I made all this up." After that quick reflection, she went off to join her little entourage of ladies-in-waiting, and found them looking for her everywhere.

All Plousine could think of that night was the choice she would have to make in the morning. She nearly resolved to pick beauty, but as she was wise enough to wish she were wiser, she finally decided that quality of mind was the gift she would ask for. She rose with the dawn and ran out to the meadow, telling everyone she wanted to pick flowers for a garland to give her mother the queen when she arose. Her attendants scattered to seek out the brightest and loveliest; the meadow was full of them. Meanwhile, the young princess ran to the riverbank and found a perfect column of white marble at the spot where she had seen the fairy the day before. After a moment the column opened and the fairy emerged, no longer a fish but rather a tall, radiant, majestic woman, her hair and her gown strewn with gemstones. "I am Anguillette," she told the dumbstruck young princess, "and I have come to keep my promise. You have wished for a fine mind, and you shall have it—fine enough to merit the envy of all who think themselves wise."

With that young Plousine felt a great change come over her, and when she thanked the fairy she spoke with an eloquence she had never known before. The fairy smiled to see the princess so astounded at her own words. "I am so glad of your choice," continued Anguillette, "so delighted that you chose intelligence over the beauty so prized by people your age, that as a reward I will give you the very beauty that you so wisely spurned today. Come back tomorrow at the same time; you have until then to decide what sort of beauty you wish for."

The fairy vanished, leaving young Plousine even happier than she had been before; the wish to improve her mind was the work of her reason, but the promise of beauty pleased her heart, and what pleases the heart always moves us the most. The young princess came back from the riverbank to collect the flowers her ladies-in-waiting had gathered. She fashioned a very pretty garland and took it to her mother; but great was the queen's surprise, and the king's, and the entire court's, when they heard young Plousine speak with an elegance that captivated every heart! Her sisters struggled mightily to find her less intelligent than the all the others around her, but in vain: they could not repress their amazement or restrain their admiration.

Night fell; her thoughts full of her future beauty, the princess did not go to bed but made for a little room in the palace, a room on whose walls hung portraits of the queens and princesses of her house, all of them depicted as goddesses, each more beautiful than the last. A study of these portraits, hoped the princess, would surely help her choose a kind of beauty worthy of being sought from the fairy.

Her eye first landed on a blond Juno,[2] with an air befitting the queen of the gods; Pallas[3] and Venus stood

---

2. Juno was a Roman goddess: queen of the Olympian gods, goddess of marriage, protector of women.

3. Pallas [Athena]: often used as an epithet for the goddess Athena. Pallas, daughter of Triton, was the close friend of Athena, daughter of

beside her, for that painting depicted the Judgment of Paris.[4] The young princess admired Pallas's proud nobility, but the lovely Venus seemed sure to emerge the victor. Plousine went on to the next canvas, which showed Pomona[5] half reclining on a bed of grass, under trees laden with the prettiest fruits in the world; she seemed so charming that the princess, who since that morning knew everything, was in no way surprised that a god had taken on many forms just to please her. Next came Diana,[6] precisely as the poets depict her: a quiver on her back and a bow in her hand, she was chasing a deer, followed by a large troupe of nymphs. A little further on, Flora[7] drew the princess's eye, strolling among flowers whose blooms, wonderful though they were, paled next to her fair skin. Next came the Graces, elegant and delightful; that painting was the last in the row.

But the princess was struck by another portrait. This one was hung over the fireplace, and showed the goddess of youth; a divine air suffused her entire person, her hair was the finest blond in the world, her face was

---

Zeus. After Pallas was killed by Athena in an accident, Athena was associated with her much-regretted friend by this epithet.

4. Paris of Troy had to name one of the three rival goddesses as most beautiful.

5. Pomona: Roman goddess of fruits and abundance.

6. Diana: Roman goddess of the hunt. She is often portrayed with a quiver and bow in Ovid's *Metamorphoses*.

7. Flora: Roman goddess of flowers, of vegetable growth, and of spring.

harmoniously shaped, her mouth charming, her bust perfectly formed, and her eyes seemed apt to trouble a man's reason even more than the nectar with which she was merrily filling a cup. "I want," cried the young princess after she had studied that splendid portrait, "I want to be as beautiful as Hebe, and to stay so for many years, if such a thing is possible." Once she had made that wish she returned to her room, where the dawn she so eagerly awaited seemed to her far too slow in coming.

But finally it did come, and she went back to the riverbank. The fairy was true to her word: she appeared by the water and splashed a few drops on Plousine's face. Instantly the princess became as beautiful as she had hoped. A number of sea gods had accompanied the fairy, and their applause was the first effect of happy Plousine's charms. She looked at herself in the water and could scarcely recognize herself; her speechlessness alone expressed the depth of her gratitude. "I have fulfilled all your wishes," said the generous fairy, "and you should be happy, but for my part I will not be, not until my gifts have surpassed your every desire. I have given you beauty and a good mind; now I will give you all the treasures in my possession, of which there is no end. Whenever you like, you need only wish for it, and at once you will have riches beyond measure, for yourself and for anyone you think worthy of them."

The fairy disappeared, and young Plousine, now as beautiful as Hebe, returned to the palace, charming everyone she encountered. Her entrance was announced in the court; the king himself was stunned by her beauty, recognizing her only by her voice and her manner. She informed the king that a fairy had given her these precious gifts, and with that everyone took to calling her Hebe, because she so perfectly resembled that goddess's magnificent portrait. What fresh reasons to hate her all this gave her sisters! They envied her intelligence less than her beauty. Every prince who had once been stirred by their charms now abruptly forgot them, and every other beauty of the court was similarly forsaken. Tears and reproaches had no effect on their inconstant lovers—a most shocking thing at the time, but one that seems to have become an established custom sometime since. Everyone around Hebe burned with love, but her heart was unmoved.

Despite her sisters' hatred, there was nothing she did not do to please them; she wished so many treasures on the older one—and for her wishing and giving were one and the same—that the grandest king of that region asked for her hand, and married her with dazzling splendor. Hebe's father sent an army out on a campaign; the beautiful princess's wishes caused his every stratagem to succeed, and his kingdom reaped a vast fortune that made him the most formidable of all kings.

But Hebe wearied of the busy life of the court, and decided to retire for a few months to a cozy house not far from the capital city. She had stripped that abode of any trace of luxury, but everything about it was charmingly simple and tasteful. The surrounding promenades were decorated by nature alone, untouched by artifice, for all around that delightful retreat lay a wood traversed by winding, half-wild roads and little brooks that tumbled and splashed in natural cascades.

Young Hebe often went out to stroll in that secluded wood; one day she felt a boredom and a yearning that swelled in her heart and would not go away. In hopes of determining the cause, she sat down on the grass by a stream whose soft murmur harmonized with her pensive mood. "What sorrow," she asked herself, "has come to trouble my perfect happiness? In all the universe, what princess enjoys a contentment as entire as mine? Thanks to that kindhearted fairy I have everything I've ever desired: I can heap gifts on everyone around me, no one I see fails to adore me, and I have only tranquility in my heart. No, I can't think what might be causing the intolerable boredom that's been spoiling my pleasures of late."

The princess could not stop pondering that question. Finally she resolved to go to the bank of Anguillette's river in the hope that she might see her. Used to fulfilling the princess's wishes, the fairy immediately appeared at the surface of the water, for this was one of those days when she took the form of a fish.

"I am always happy to see you, young princess," she said to Hebe. "I know you have been staying lately in a peaceful and secluded place, but you seem to be feeling a disquiet that scarcely suits your fortune. What might be wrong, Hebe? Confide in me."

"Nothing is wrong," the young princess answered uncomfortably. "You have given me so much—what could be missing from a happiness you created with your own hands?"

"Come now, you're not being honest," the fairy answered. "Your melancholy is all too plain to see, but what more can you possibly want? Prove yourself worthy of my kindness with a simple confession," added the gracious fairy, "and I promise to fulfill your wishes once again."

"I don't know what I want," charming Hebe answered; then, lowering her beautiful eyes, she went on, "and yet I can't help but feel that something is lacking, something absolutely essential to my happiness."

"Ah!" cried the fairy, "what you want is love, for only desire can give rise to thoughts as senseless as those. A dangerous thing, is desire!" the prudent fairy continued. "You want love, and you shall have it—every heart is all too keen to take it—but I warn you, when you want me to put an end to that fatal passion you believe to be so sweet a joy, you will invoke me in vain. My powers do not go so far as that."[8]

---

8. The pessimistic and cynical view of love implied by the author here is a common theme in Murat as well as in other *contes* of the late seventeenth century.

"No matter," the young princess quickly answered, smiling and blushing at the same time. "Why, what use are the gifts you have given me, if not to make another as happy as I?"

The fairy sighed to hear those words, and dove once more underwater. Hebe went back to her solitude full of an expectancy that was already beginning to ease her boredom; she felt some concern at the fairy's warning, but those sensible reflections were soon chased away by other thoughts, more dangerous but more agreeable. In her house she found a letter from the king, summoning her back to the palace at once, so that she might be present at a festival planned for the next day.

A few hours later, she set off for the court; the king and queen received her with pleasure, then told her a traveling prince had recently arrived from abroad, and they wanted to show him a festival so that as his journey continued he might tell far and wide of the magnificence he had seen in their kingdom.

Full of a presentiment she had never felt before, Hebe asked her sister the princess if this stranger was agreeable to look on.

"We've never seen anything like him," she answered.

"Describe him," said Hebe, trembling with emotion.

"He is exactly as heroes are portrayed," Ilérie told her. "His chest is beautiful, his air is great, his eyes are full of a fire whose power has stirred more than one aloof woman of this court. He has the finest head in the world, his hair is more black than blond, and he need only show himself to rivet the attention of all those who see him."

"A very appealing portrait," answered young Hebe. "Is it perhaps just a little too glowing?"

"It is not, sister," Princess Ilérie answered with a sigh she could not hold back. "Oh! you may find him far too worthy of your love."

That evening, the prince appeared in the queen's rooms and asked to be introduced to the beautiful Hebe, whom he had yet to meet; never were two hearts so suddenly or so deeply moved, nor did two hearts ever have so many good reasons to be. Their conversation involved only trivial matters, but it was lively and pleasant, and fueled by a vigorous desire to please.

The queen soon retired, and beautiful Hebe, left to reflect on her sentiments, realized she had lost all her tranquility of spirit, something whose preciousness she had never realized before. "Anguillette," she cried to herself once she was alone, "oh! what a man you have allowed to offer himself to my gaze! His presence has erased all your wise words. Why did you not give me the strength to resist such enticing charms? But perhaps their power is greater even than a fairy's."

Hebe slept little that night; she rose early, and the need to ready herself for the evening's festivities occupied her all day with an urgency she had never felt before, because for the first time in her life she wanted to draw someone to her. Full of the same desire, the young stranger spared no effort to make himself seem loveworthy in charming Hebe's eyes. Nor did Princess Ilérie neglect any detail that might tickle a young man's fancy; she was a woman graced with a thousand charms, and without Hebe by her side she seemed the most beautiful creature alive, but when Hebe was there she was entirely eclipsed. That evening the queen threw an elegant ball, with a lavish feast to follow; the young stranger would have remarked on the prodigious luxury of it all had he been able to look at something other than Hebe. After the meal, a novel illumination filled the palace garden with dazzling lights. It was summertime, and everyone came out to enjoy an evening stroll. The handsome stranger had the queen on his arm, but that honor was no consolation for the misery of having to spend a few moments away from his princess. The trees were festooned with flowers, and the lights of the illumination were arranged to depict a profusion of bows, arrows, and all the rest of love's arsenal. Here and there they spelled out a few lines of writing.

In a small grove lit like the rest of the gardens, the queen sat down beside a pretty fountain ringed with rustic seats draped in carnations and roses; while the queen talked with the king and the crowd of courtiers surrounding them, the princesses gazed at the images made by the little lights. The handsome stranger was close by Hebe's side. She turned her gaze toward a depiction of arrows and read aloud these words, which were written beneath them:

Some arrows are invincible.

"Those are the ones that shoot from divine Hebe's eyes," the stranger murmured, looking at her tenderly. The princess heard him, and she blushed, but to the prince her unease augured well for his love, as he detected no anger in it.

The party ended with a thousand new pleasures; the stranger's charms had moved Ilérie's heart too deeply for her not to grasp at once that he loved another. Before Hebe's arrival at court, the prince had been attentive to Ilérie; now he was occupied with his new feelings alone, striving at every moment to touch the beautiful princess's heart. He was in love, and he was worthy of love; fate was driving Hebe to love him, and the fairy had given her permission to follow her heart: so many excuses to surrender! In the end, she found she could combat her feelings no longer.

The charming stranger had told her he was the son of a king, and his name was Atimir; that name was known to the princess, for he who bore it had performed wondrous feats of bravery in a long-ago war between the two kingdoms. Those two realms had always been foes, and so the prince had first presented himself at the court of Hebe's father under a different name. After a conversation in which her heart finally drank down all the sweet, dangerous poison the fairy had spoken of, the young princess gave Atimir leave to reveal his rank and his love to the king. The prince joyously ran off to the king's rooms, and spoke to him with all the ardor inspired by his tender emotions. The king took him to see the queen; since this marriage would bring lasting peace to the kingdom, it was promised that beautiful Hebe would wed her happy suitor as soon as he received his father's consent. That news soon spread, and Princess Ilérie succumbed to a sorrow every bit as consuming as her jealousy: she wept, she moaned, but she had no choice but to contain herself, and to conceal regrets that could do nothing to help her.

Beautiful Hebe and Atimir were now together at every possible moment. Their love grew greater every day, and the young princess wondered why fairies who wanted to make mortals happy did not simply let them know love. An ambassador dispatched by Atimir's father then arrived at the court, bringing a breathlessly awaited announcement: the king approved of his son's marriage to Hebe. Preparations for the wedding were begun at once. Now Atimir felt he had nothing to fear—a most dangerous way for a lover to feel, if one wants to keep him forever faithful.

The prince became less attentive to Hebe once his happiness was assured. One day he was out looking for her in the palace gardens and heard women's voices coming from a little hut tucked among the honeysuckles; he heard his name spoken, and he was curious to know more. He tiptoed toward the hut and clearly made out Princess Ilérie's voice: "I will die before that terrible day comes, my dear Cléonice," she was telling the young woman sitting next to her. "The gods will not force me to see the ingrate I love united with lucky Hebe. My torment is too terrible; I will not survive much longer."

"But Madame," answered the girl, "Prince Atimir never betrayed you: he never offered you his heart at all. Your misfortune is simply the workings of fate. And with all the many princes who love you, you would surely find someone finer than he if only your heart were not so embittered."

"Finer than he?" answered Ilérie. "Can there be such a thing, in all the universe? O powerful fairy," she added with a sigh, "of all the gifts you have given Hebe, I am now jealous of only one: the tender love Atimir feels for her."

Here the princess's words were cut short by her sobs. How happy she would have been had she known how they moved Atimir's heart! She stood up to leave the hut, and the prince took cover behind a clump of trees; Ilérie's tears and passionate tone had stirred him deeply, but he told himself he was simply sorry for a beautiful princess whose feelings he had unintentionally hurt. He went off and found Hebe, whose charms immediately silenced every other memory in his heart.

Crossing through the gardens to accompany her to the palace, he spied something lying at his feet. He picked it up and saw that it was a magnificent little notebook. The hut where he had overheard Ilérie's words was not far away; he feared that if he showed Hebe the notebook she might learn of those events. He hid it away, unseen by the princess, for just then she was busy resetting a pin in her hair.

Ilérie did not appear in the queen's apartments that evening; word had it that she'd taken ill on the way home from her walk. Atimir knew full well that she was trying to conceal the distress she'd revealed in the hut, and his pity for her grew all the greater.

The moment he was back in his rooms, he opened the notebook he had found; on the first page he saw a cipher composed of a double *A* crowned with myrtle and held up by little Cupids, one trying to dry his tears with his drape, another breaking his arrows in two. The sight of that cipher brought about a rush of emotion in the young prince; he knew that Ilérie could draw beautifully, and he quickly turned the page in search of further enlightenment. On the back of the sheet, he found these words:

Almighty Love showed me your charms,
And now my heart will never be at peace again.
O cruel man, how can you be so unjust?
You use me to practice firing the arrows
With which you mean to wound another.

Recognizing her hand, he now knew all too well that this was Princess Ilérie's notebook, and he was touched by the depth of her emotion, an emotion unprompted by any attention he had shown her, unsupported even by hope. Reading those lines, he recalled that he had been drawn to Ilérie before Hebe had appeared at court; he began to believe he had betrayed Princess Ilérie, and so he did indeed betray charming Hebe. He struggled against his impulse, but his heart was prone to inconstancy, and that dangerous habit is a hard one to break. He dropped Ilérie's notebook onto a table, determined never to give it another glance, but a moment later he could not help but pick it up again, and as he read he found a thousand things that guaranteed Ilérie's triumph over the divine Hebe.

All night long, the prince's heart was tormented by a thousand tangled emotions; the next morning he went to see the king, who named the date he had chosen for Atimir's wedding with Hebe. The prince answered with a stammer that the king took for a sign of his love. How little we know the hearts of men! It was nothing other than an effect of his faithlessness. The king wanted to visit the queen, and the prince had no choice but to follow him. Princess Ilérie came in soon after; seeing her downcast air, and no longer ignorant of the cause, the inconstant Atimir found her more appealing than ever. He approached her and spoke to her for some time, making it clear that he was not unaware of her feelings. He tenderly begged her forgiveness, bringing Ilérie a joy that was almost more than she could bear. Oh! how to withstand so overwhelming a happiness, and one so long awaited?

At that moment sweet Hebe arrived at the queen's apartments; Princess Ilérie and fickle Atimir blushed at the sight of her. "How beautiful she is!" said Ilérie, looking at the prince with an anxiety she could not hide. "Flee her, my lord, or else put an end to my life at last." The prince could not answer; Hebe had approached, full of a grace and a charm that delivered a thousand rebukes to the thankless Atimir. Unable to endure it, he took his leave of the princess, saying he had to dispatch a courier to his father. Such was her faith in Atimir that she did not even see that he glanced more than once at Ilérie. As Ilérie secretly rejoiced at that, the beautiful Hebe learned from the king and queen that in three days' time she would be Atimir's wife. How unworthy he was of the sentiments this news summoned up in lovely Hebe's heart! Preoccupied though he was with his new, faithless ardor, the prince spent a part of the next day with Hebe; Ilérie saw them together, and a thousand times thought she might die of jealousy. Her love had redoubled as soon as she felt a glimmer of hope.

Returning to his apartments that evening, the prince found a stranger bearing a note. He opened it feverishly, finding these words:

> I yield to a passion a thousand times stronger than my reason, for it is now too late to conceal feelings that chance has revealed to you. Come, Prince, come and learn the decision I have made, inspired by my deep love for you. How happy I will be if it costs me only my life!

The messenger told the prince he had been charged to lead him to a place where Princess Ilérie was awaiting him; Atimir followed without a moment's hesitation, and after a long, roundabout walk he was shown into a little tent at the end of a deeply shaded forest path. In the tent's muted light he saw Ilérie alone with one of her ladies-in-waiting, while the others strolled in the garden; once she had retired to this sanctuary, they entered only on her order.

He found Ilérie sitting on a pile of scarlet cushions with golden embroidery, draped in a sumptuous gown of yellow and gold. Her magnificent black hair was held back by yellow diamond clasps and ribbons matching her gown. Seeing her, Atimir could not force himself to be ashamed of his infidelity; he knelt down before her, as Ilérie looked on him with a gaze that eloquently expressed what she felt in her heart.

"Prince," she said, "I have not asked you here to persuade you to call off your wedding; I know all too well that nothing can stop it now, and the few words with which you so kindly indulged my sadness and my affection give me no grounds to believe you might one day abandon Hebe for me. But," she went on, shedding tears that sealed the seduction of Atimir's heart, "I want nothing more to do with this life of pain and sorrow, and without regret I will sacrifice it to my love." She showed him a little golden box she held in her hand. "Thanks to this poison," she said, "I will be spared the horrible torment of seeing you become Hebe's husband."

"No, beautiful Ilérie," cried the fickle prince, "I will not be her husband. I will abandon it all for your sake, as I love you a thousand times more than I ever loved Hebe; and despite my desire and my solemn oath, I am prepared to take you to a place where nothing will stand in the way of our love."

"Ah! but prince," sighed Ilérie, "can I trust a man who has already proven untrue?"

"He will never be untrue to you," Atimir answered, "and your father the king, who gave me Hebe's hand, will not refuse me the lovely Ilérie when I have her in my hands."

"Come then, Atimir," said the princess after a few moments of silence, "let us go where our twinned fates are calling us; whatever sadness it might bring me, nothing can compete in my heart with the sweet delight of being loved by the one I love."

With this, they began to make plans for their escape. There was no time to waste, so they decided to set off the next night; that decision having been made, they reluctantly parted. Despite Atimir's promises, Ilérie still feared the effect of Hebe's charms; the rest of that night and the following day, that fear plagued her unceasingly.

Meanwhile, the prince quickly gave the necessary orders for his secret departure, and the next night, as soon as everyone had come into the palace to retire, he went off to find Ilérie in the garden tent where she was awaiting him with Cléonice. Off they rode at great speed, eager to be gone from the kingdom. The next morning, the news of their elopement was announced by a letter from Ilérie to the queen, and another from Atimir to the king: the letters were touching, and plainly dictated by love. The king and queen were outraged, but no words can express the grief of poor, charming Hebe. What despair! So many tears! So many entreaties addressed to the fairy Anguillette, asking her to put an end to sorrows that had proved every bit as cruel as she had predicted! But the fairy was true to her word; in vain did Hebe come again and again to the riverbank, Anguillette was nowhere to be seen. The princess abandoned herself to the most devastating despair. The young men of the court, once discouraged by Atimir's good fortune, now felt their hopes being reborn, but to faithful Hebe their attentions and affections were only fresh torments.

The king was determined to see her take a husband, and several times he had urged her to make her choice, but that task was too cruel for her aching heart, and she resolved to flee her father's kingdom. Before she left she went to the river one last time, hoping to see Anguillette. This time the fairy could not resist the beautiful Hebe's tears: she appeared, and on seeing her the princess sobbed all the louder, too overcome to speak. "And so at last," said the fairy, "at last you know the nature of the poisonous happiness I always tried to keep from you; but Hebe, Atimir has already punished you far too well for not heeding my counsel. Go, flee this land where everything summons up memories of your love. Go to the sea; you will find a vessel that will take you to the one place in this world where you can be cured of the unhappy love that has caused your despair. But remember," added Anguillette, more severely now, "once your heart has regained its tranquility, you must never seek Atimir's noxious presence, for that would you cost you your life."

More than once Hebe wished she could see the prince again, no matter the price Love might exact for that pleasure, but a lingering trace of good sense and a concern for her reputation convinced her to accept the fairy's suggestion. She thanked her for this final favor, and the next morning she set off for the sea, followed by her most trusted ladies-in-waiting.

She found Anguillette's boat; it was gilded from stem to stern, with masts of elaborate marquetry and sails of a silver and pink fabric that bore the word *Freedom* over and over. The crew's uniforms matched the sail, and indeed everything about the boat seemed to express the pleasures of freedom. The princess was shown to a magnificent room, with handsome furniture and exquisite paintings, but she felt no less sorrow here than in her father's court. In vain did her attendants strive to amuse her with a thousand pleasures; she was not yet ready to notice.

One day, studying the paintings in her room, her eye lit on a landscape in which a young shepherdess was shown merrily cutting snares to liberate a great flock of imprisoned birds, some of which, already freed, were flying up toward the heavens with wondrous speed. Every other painting depicted a similar situation; love was the subject of none of them, and they all vaunted the charms of freedom. "Oh!" cried the princess in sadness, "will my heart never feel such sweet contentment, and for whom does my reason make so many fruitless vows?" Thus did the unhappy Hebe spend her days, forever lost in thoughts of love, and wishing she could forget it.

The ship had been at sea for a month when one morning, as she was standing on the upper deck, the princess spied land in the distance. It seemed a most beautiful place: the trees were extraordinarily tall and graceful, and as the boat drew nearer she saw they were filled with birds of bright and varied plumage. The birds sang in perfect harmony; their songs were sweet, and they seemed to take care not to sing too loudly. The boat landed on that welcoming shore; the princess and ladies-in-waiting disembarked, and with her first breath of the island's air she felt her heart suddenly at peace, soothed by some unknown power. A restful slumber came over her, keeping her beautiful eyes closed for some time. That pleasant land, which she knew nothing of, was Tranquility Isle; the fairy Anguillette, a close relative of the family who reigned in that land, had two thousand years earlier endowed it with the gift of curing unhappy passions. The island still enjoys that power to this day—the difficulty is finding one's way to its shores.

The reigning monarch was a direct descendent of the celebrated Princess Carpillon[9] and her charming husband, whose wondrous deeds have been so elegantly recounted to us by a modern fairy, wiser and more polished than those of antiquity. While Hebe enjoyed a rest

---

9. Reference to the fairy tale "Princesse Carpillon" by Murat's contemporary Marie-Catherine d'Aulnoy.

sweeter than any she had known for six months, the prince of Tranquility Isle had come out for a drive in the woods by the seashore; he sat in a carriage pulled by four young white elephants, accompanied by a host of courtiers. The sleeping princess caught his eye, and he was astonished by her beauty. He alighted from his carriage with an eagerness he had never felt before. One glimpse of Hebe had filled him with all the love her charms deserved to inspire. Awakened by the sound of his approach, she opened her eyes, showing the prince a thousand new beauties. He was the same age as Hebe, for he was then nineteen years old, a resplendent young man graced from head to toe with a thousand charms. He was taller than an ordinary man, and his hair, which fell in thick curls to his belt, was the same color as Hebe's. His gown was made entirely of feathers, in a thousand varied colors, and over it he wore a long mantle of swan feathers, clasped at the shoulders by the finest gems in the world. His belt was made of diamonds, and a little ruby-encrusted dagger hung from it by two chains. He was coiffed with a sort of helmet, made with feathers like the rest of his garb, ornamented on one side by heron plumes held in place by an enormous diamond, which lent him a tremendous grace. The prince was the first sight the young princess spied on awaking; she thought him worthy of her gaze, and for the first time in her life she looked at someone other than Atimir with a certain attention.

"Everything about you assures me," said the prince of Tranquility Isle to the princess, "that you must be none other than the divine Hebe. Oh! who else could have so many charms?"

"But, my lord," the young princess answered, blushing as she rose to her feet, "who could have told you I was here on this island?"

"A powerful fairy," the young king answered, "who, wanting to make me the happiest prince in the world, and this land the most blessed, had promised me that she would bring you here, and even allowed me to dream still more glorious dreams. But," he added with a sigh, "I know full well that my fate will depend far more on your kindness than on hers."

She answered these words most elegantly, and the prince invited her to climb into his carriage to be taken to the palace; out of respect, he did not want to sit down beside her, but since she had understood from his words and his entourage that he was the king of this island, she insisted he sit at her side. Never had such a beautiful couple been seen in a single carriage: the prince's courtiers could not help but break into thunderous applause. As they rode, the young prince engaged Hebe in a very courtly and sensitive conversation, and the princess, overjoyed to find her heart at peace again, felt her good cheer returning.

They arrived at the palace, not far from the shoreline. Long, graceful avenues led to it, past canals of limpid, quick-flowing water. The palace was built entirely of ivory, and covered in agate. In every courtyard the prince's guards stood lined up in ranks; in the first, they were dressed in yellow feathers and equipped with quivers, bows, and silver arrows, while in the second they wore orange feathers and bore gold-filigreed sabers adorned with turquoise. Next came the third courtyard, where the guards were dressed in white feathers and held painted and gilded spontoons[10] draped with flowers. War was unknown in that land, so there was no need for deadly weapons. The prince descended from his carriage and led the lovely Hebe into a magnificent hall. There were a great many courtiers; the ladies were beautiful, the men charming and strong, and although everyone in that land dressed in nothing but feathers, they showed a rare talent for arranging those plumes to take full advantage of their varied tints, which made of them a most handsome people.

That evening, the prince of Tranquility Isle gave a superb feast in Hebe's honor, followed by a concert played on soft flutes, lutes, theorboes, and cembalos:[11] no instrument of piercing tone was allowed in that land. The melody was most gracious, and after it had gone on for some time, a lovely voice sang out these words:

---

10. A spontoon is a short pike, here of a purely ceremonial nature.
11. A theorbo is a type of bass lute, and a cembalo is a harpsichord.

> I swear immortal ardor for your charms;
> What happiness could be sweeter
> Than the joy of bearing so lovely a chain?
> My love will be tender, my heart will be true,
> And my reward will depend only on you.

The prince looked at Hebe as these words were sung, his gaze tender enough to convince her that he was thinking exactly what he was hearing in those lines.

It was late when the music was over, and so the prince of Tranquility Isle escorted the princess to her rooms, which were the finest in the palace. She found a host of ladies-in-waiting, on whom the prince had bestowed the honor of attending her. When he left the beautiful Hebe, he was more in love than any man can be. The ladies helped the princess to bed, then withdrew, leaving only those the princess had brought with her.

"Who would ever have thought it?" she said to them once they were alone. "My heart is at peace! What god has calmed my torments? I no longer love Atimir; I can tell myself that he may be Ilérie's husband by now and not die of grief. Is all this nothing more than a dream? No, not even my dreams are so peaceful." Then she offered up a thousand thanks to Anguillette, and went to sleep.

The next morning she opened her bed-curtains to find the fairy standing there before her, wearing a benevolent expression Hebe had not seen since that terrible day when she asked her to let her know love. "In the end, I brought you to this place, and it's a good thing I did," said the good fairy. "Your heart is free, and so it will be happy. I have cured you of a cruel passion, but, Hebe, can I trust the horrible torments you have endured to assure me that for the rest of your life you will avoid any place where you might see the ungrateful Atimir again?"

What would the young princess not promise the fairy? How many oaths she swore against love and her unfaithful lover!

"Just remember your promises," answered Anguillette, with an air that commanded respect. "Should you ever try to see him again, you will die by Atimir's side; but everything on this island will cure you of that dangerous desire. I will hide from you no more that I have made a decision in your favor: the prince of Tranquility Isle is my relative, and I am the protector of his person and his empire. He is young and fine, and no prince in the world is so worthy of being your husband. Reign, then, beautiful Hebe, reign over his heart and his kingdom. Your father has given his consent; I was in his palace only yesterday, and I told him and your mother the queen where you are; they placed you entirely in my hands."

The princess yearned to ask the fairy what news she had heard of Ilérie and Atimir, but after so many favors she did not dare take the risk of displeasing her. She used all the eloquence Anguillette had given her to express her profound thanks.

A knock came at the door, and the fairy disappeared before Hebe's attendants entered. As soon as Hebe had risen, twelve beautiful children, dressed as Cupids, brought her twelve crystal baskets filled with the most beautiful and agreeable flowers in the world, a gift from the prince. Beneath those flowers, the baskets were filled with the most marvelous gems, in every conceivable color. In the first basket she found a note with these words:

> To the divine Hebe,
> Yesterday I swore my love to you a thousand
>   times,
> Promises inspired by my undying love,
> Dictated by love itself,
> Whose memory I will never forget,
> And your charms will assure that they are kept.

Remembering the fairy's decree, she knew she should receive her new lover's attentions as those of a prince who would soon be her husband. She graciously welcomed the little cupids, and she had hardly given them leave to go when twenty-four dwarves, curiously but magnificently attired, appeared with yet more presents: feather gowns whose colors, stitching, and gemstones were so lovely that the princess admitted she had never seen the like. She chose a pink one to put on for the day, and her hair was adorned with a matching bouquet of feathers. She looked so charming with this new ornament that the prince of Tranquility Isle, who came to see her as soon as she was dressed, felt his passion leap even higher than before. The entire court came to admire the princess. When evening fell, the prince suggested to the beautiful Hebe that they go out to the palace gardens, which were a wonderful sight to behold.

As they strolled the prince recounted to Hebe that the fairy had foretold her arrival on Tranquility Isle four years earlier. "But after some time had gone by," the prince added, "when I asked when her promise would come true, she grew sad and answered, 'Princess Hebe's father wants to give her to another, but unless I am greatly mistaken she will never belong to the prince he has chosen. I will tell you more when the time comes.' A few months later, the fairy returned to our island. 'Destiny has smiled on you,' she told me. 'The prince who was to be Hebe's husband will not be after all, and you will soon see the most beautiful princess in the world here on your shores.'"

"It is true," Hebe answered with a blush, "that I was to marry a prince from a kingdom neighboring my father's, but in the end it was my sister he loved, and it was her he took back to his land."

The prince of Tranquility Isle offered a thousand well-turned remarks on Hebe's happy fate, which had brought her to his island just as the fairy had said. She listened with pleasure, all the more because his speech had interrupted her account of her adventures; she feared that she might not be able to discuss her unfaithful lover without revealing just how fond of him she had been.

The prince of Tranquility Isle led Hebe to a richly ornamented grotto, made still prettier by magnificent fountains. The depths of the grotto were dark; there were many niches filled with statues of shepherds and nymphs, scarcely visible in the dimness. After a few moments the princess heard an agreeable music: all at once a bright illumination came to life, and the princess could see that some of the statues made up the orchestra, while the others came and danced a most elegant and artistic ballet before her, sometimes breaking into sweet, tender song. Every actor in this divertissement had thus been concealed deep in this grotto for the sole sake of giving the princess a delightful surprise. Once the ballet was over, native servants brought in a superb repast, and dinner was served beneath a pergola of jasmine and orange flowers.

These festivities had just ended when the fairy Anguillette appeared in the air, riding a chariot yoked to four monkeys.[12] Coming to earth, she announced the good news to the prince: she wanted him to be Hebe's husband, and the beautiful princess had given her con-

---

12. The Champion edition reads "cygnes," or swans (Murat, "Anguillette" 107).

sent. The prince was so overcome with joy that he did not know whom to thank first, Hebe or Anguillette, and although the words inspired by joy are never as moving as those born of sorrow, he acquitted himself with wit and grace. The fairy planned to stay with the prince and the princess until their wedding, three days hence; she lavished fine gifts on the beautiful Hebe and the prince of Tranquility Isle, and when the day came the three of them made their way together to the matrimonial temple, accompanied by the entire court and a vast crowd of the island's inhabitants.

That temple was built entirely of interlaced olive and palm branches, which by the power of the fairy never lost their greenery. The goddess of marriage was represented by a white marble statue, crowned with roses; she stood on an altar ornamented only with flowers, and beside her was a little Cupid, merrily presenting her with a crown of myrtles. Anguillette, who had created this temple, wanted everything about it to be simple, in order to express that love is all that is needed for a happy marriage. The only difficulty is bringing love and marriage together—a miracle truly worthy of a fairy! And on Tranquility Isle she had joined them forever, for there—unlike any other kingdom on earth—one could be both a spouse and a lover, and remain true to the end.

In that temple, the beautiful Hebe, under Anguillette's guidance, pledged her faith to the prince of Tranquility

Isle and received his vows with pleasure. She did not feel
for him the overpowering love she had once felt for Atimir; but her heart, now rid of passion, accepted that husband on the fairy's command, as a prince worthy of her
by his beauty, and even more by his love. Their union
was celebrated with a thousand elegant festivities, and
Hebe found herself happy with a prince who adored her.

Meanwhile, Hebe's father the king had received a
team of ambassadors dispatched by Atimir, who sought
his permission to wed Ilérie. Atimir's father had died;
the kingdom was now his, and he was joyfully accorded
the princess he had spirited away. After their wedding,
Queen Ilérie sent another group of ambassadors to her
parents' court, to ask if she could come home and beg
their forgiveness for a misstep inspired by love alone,
one that could surely be excused on the grounds of
Atimir's merit. The king granted his permission, and
Atimir accompanied her; the day of their arrival was celebrated with a thousand amusements. Soon after, the
beautiful Hebe and her charming husband sent their
own ambassadors to the king and queen, to announce
the news of their marriage; Anguillette had already informed them, but the ambassadors were nonetheless received with pleasure and pomp. Atimir was with the
king when they presented themselves; the fond thought
of Hebe could never be wholly erased from a heart over
which it had reigned so imperiously. Atimir could not

hold back a sigh on hearing of the good fortune of the prince of Tranquility Isle; he went so far as to accuse Hebe of infidelity, never thinking how many reasons he had given her to forsake him.

The prince's ambassadors returned home, laden with honors and gifts; they told their prince and princess of the king and queen's great joy at the news of their happy marriage. But—oh, the perils of an account too complete!— they also told Hebe that they had seen Atimir and Ilérie at the court. Those names, so dangerous for her peace of mind, filled her with deep agitation; she was happy, but can a mortal remain perfectly happy forever?

She could not stifle her impatience to be back in the king's court; she told herself it was her father she wanted to see, as well as her mother the queen, and indeed she believed it. How often, when we love, do our own feelings deceive us! Despite the fairy's command to avoid any place where she might find Atimir, she suggested to the prince of Tranquility Isle that they make the trip. At first he refused; Anguillette had forbidden him to let Hebe leave his kingdom. She continued to plead; he adored her; he knew nothing of the passion she had once felt for Atimir: who among us can say no to the one we love? He told himself that his unquestioning indulgence would make Hebe happy; he gave orders to set sail, and never had there been such a sight as his ships and his entourage. Indignant to see Hebe and the prince disobeying her order, wise

Anguillette abandoned them to their fate, and gave them no further counsel, since they had learned so little from it.

The prince and the princess boarded their ship, and after a pleasant journey they arrived at the court of Hebe's father. The king and queen felt a deep joy on seeing the beautiful princess again; they were charmed by the prince of Tranquility Isle, and they celebrated the couple's arrival with a thousand festivities all through the kingdom, but Ilérie trembled to learn that Hebe had returned. It was decided that they would meet and say nothing more of all that had happened.

Atimir asked to see Hebe again—a little too eagerly, thought Ilérie. Princess Hebe blushed when he entered her room, and both found themselves in a state of disquiet from which all their wit could not free them. The king, who was present, did not fail to notice; he joined their conversation, and to cut it short he invited the princess to come visit the gardens. Atimir did not dare give his arm to Hebe; he bade her a respectful goodbye and withdrew. But what ideas and emotions did he bear away in his heart! All the fierce, tender passion he had once felt for Hebe was reawakened in an instant; he hated Ilérie, and he hated himself. Never was an unfaithful thought followed by so much remorse, or so much sorrow.

That evening he was in the queen's rooms, as was Princess Hebe. He had eyes only for her, and sought out every opportunity to talk with her. She slipped away every time, but she could not be at peace: his gaze spoke for him all too clearly. The days went by, and his every action continued to show her that her eyes had regained their power over him. Hebe's heart was alarmed, for Atimir still seemed in every way worthy of her love; she resolved to shun him as vigorously as she had sought him. She spoke to him only in the company of the queen, and only when she could not possibly avoid it. She resolved to tell the prince of Tranquility Isle that she wanted to go home to their kingdom—but how many obstacles suddenly arise when we must leave the one we love!

One evening, preoccupied with that thought, she closed herself up in her study, where she could dream more freely, and found a note that had been secretly slipped into her pocket. She opened it, and was more moved than words can say on recognizing Atimir's handwriting. She told herself not to look, but her heart won out over her reason, and so she read these words:

> You greet my love with a heart of stone;
> Indifference is all you feel.
> Beautiful Hebe, now it is your heart that is faithless;
> For it perfectly mirrors my fateful inconstancy,
> Oh! would that it could imitate my change.
>
> Gone are those happy days
> When you deigned to share my pleasures and
>   my pains;

> We were, it is true, faithless by turns,
> But I have come back to you, still bound by the
>   same chains:
> Alas! can you not imitate my change?

"O cruel man!" cried the princess, "what did I ever do to you that you seek to reawaken in my soul an affection that has brought me so much sadness?" And with that, Hebe's words were cut short by her sobs.

Meanwhile, Ilérie was in the throes of an all too well-founded jealousy. Caught up in his passion, Atimir could no longer contain his feelings: the prince of Tranquility Isle began to sense his love for Hebe, but he wanted to study Atimir's conduct further before speaking of it to the princess, for he loved her as deeply as ever, and he feared that his own words might awaken her to Atimir's passion.

A few days after Hebe had received that letter, a joust was held, with the princes and all the fine youth of the court competing in honor of the ladies. The king and queen graced that event with their presence, and the beautiful Hebe and Princess Ilérie were to give out the prizes: one was a sword whose guard and scabbard were covered with jewels of extraordinary beauty, the other a wristlet of perfect, sparkling diamonds. All the knights listed for the races were magnificently arrayed, mounted on the finest horses in the world; they wore the colors of their mistresses, and their shields bore devices rich in meaning, expressive of the sentiments in their hearts.

Riding a black-maned horse of incomparable beauty, the prince of Tranquility Isle appeared, gloriously attired and equipped in brilliant pink, the color Hebe loved best. A bouquet of matching plumes fluttered above his light helmet. He drew the applause of every spectator, and he was so beautiful in his dazzling finery that Hebe secretly reproached herself a thousand times for the sentiments her sad fate inspired her to feel for another. His large entourage was dressed in the fashion of his land. Everything about them was splendid and gallant; a squire carried his shield, and everyone in the crowd peered intently to make out its device: a heart pierced by an arrow, with a little Cupid firing many more arrows in hopes of inflicting fresh wounds, but apart from the first they were all fired in vain. Beneath that image were written these words:

No other do I fear.

His colors and device made it quite clear that he had entered this contest as the champion of the beautiful Hebe.

All eyes were upon him, relishing his beauty, when suddenly Atimir appeared astride a proud black stallion. He was attired in dull brown, the color of dead leaves, unadorned by gold, silver, or gemstones; his helmet was topped by a bouquet of rose-colored plumes, and although he had affected a great negligence in his dress, he was so handsome, so assured, and rode with such grace that no one could look away from him as soon as he entered. He carried his own shield, which depicted a Cupid bound in heavy chains even as he scornfully trampled other chains underfoot. The Cupid was ringed with these words:

The only ones worthy of me.

Atimir's entourage, composed of all the principal figures of his court, was dressed in dull brown and silver, and they had not spared the gemstones. Grand though they were, it was clear from Atimir's air that he was born to command them.

No words can express the depth of the emotion roused in Hebe and Ilérie by the sight of Atimir, nor the jealousy of the prince of Tranquility Isle on seeing plumes the same color as his own fluttering atop Atimir's helmet. The device compounded his fury; if he did not act on it then and there, it was only to better choose the moment when his rival would feel his wrath. Atimir's boldness and impudence did not escape the king and queen; they were greatly vexed, but this was not the time to show it.

A thousand resounding trumpets announced the start of the joust. All the young knights showed their skill, and the competition was a fine thing to see. Even with a furious jealousy troubling his mind, the prince of Tranquility Isle distinguished himself by his skill, and emerged triumphant. Atimir knew that the first prize was to be given by Ilérie, and so chose not to challenge the prince's victory. The judges formally declared the prince the winner, and to the sound of cheers and acclamations from every spectator he came forward with great grace to receive the diamond wristlet. Princess Ilérie presented it to him; he took it respectfully, and then, having saluted the king, the queen, and the princesses, he returned to the sidelines. Poor Ilérie had all too clearly seen fickle Atimir's lack of interest in a prize that would be given by her hand, and she let out a sorrowful sigh; meanwhile, beautiful Hebe was feeling a secret joy, from which all her reason could not shield her heart.

The jousts resumed with the same outcome as before. Spurred on by the sight of Hebe, the prince of Tranquility Isle performed magnificently and was declared the winner for the second time; but Atimir, infuriated to have been reduced to a spectator of his rival's glory, and motivated by the thought of receiving a prize from Hebe's hand, took up a challenger's position at the far end of the field. The rivals gave each other a steely stare, and the prospect of a joust between two such great princes brought cries of joy from the crowd and caused a fresh surge in the two princesses' hearts. The princes raced toward each other, equally matched; they splintered their lances but were not thrown from their saddles. The applause doubled, and the princes, allowing their horses no time to catch their breath, returned to their starting points. They took up new lances, and ran just as skillfully as before, with precisely the same results.

Reluctant to see fortune name a victor, knowing that one of these two noble rivals would take umbrage, the king quickly sent word to the princes, urging them to be content with the glory they had earned and to consider the jousting done for the day. They heard out the king's envoy with some impatience, especially Atimir, who was the first to speak: "You may tell the king that I would be unworthy of the honor he does me with his concern for my good name if I allowed another man to defeat me."

"Let us see," answered the prince of Tranquility Isle, "which of us is more deserving of the favors of fortune and the king's esteem."

The envoy was not yet at the king's side when the two rivals, animated by sentiments stronger than any desire to take home the prize, reached the end of their course. Fortune favored the bold Atimir, and he was the victor. Weary from the many magnificent charges it had made, the prince of Tranquility Isle's horse collapsed to the ground, throwing its master from his saddle. What joy for Atimir, and what rage for the luckless prince! He quickly rose to his feet and hurried to his rival before anyone had approached: "You have beaten me in a game, Atimir," he said, in a tone that clearly expressed his fury, "but I would prefer to settle our differences with a sword."[13]

"Very well," answered proud Atimir. "I will await you at dawn tomorrow, in the woods at the end of the palace gardens."

The judges arrived at their side just as this exchange was ending, and the princes mutually concealed their anger, for fear that the king would oppose their plan.

The prince of Tranquility Isle climbed back on his horse and spurred it away, so as to put the fateful scene of Atimir's triumph behind him. Meanwhile, Atimir went off to receive the prize from Hebe's hand. She presented it to him with a tremulous air that betrayed the emotions roiling her soul, and as he accepted it Atimir showed all the overwrought signs of a man deeply in love. The watchful king and queen did not fail to see it, and they returned to the palace unhappy with the way this day had ended. His heart consumed with his passion, Atimir left the field alone, forbidding anyone in his entourage to accompany him; meanwhile, Ilérie returned to her rooms tormented by sadness and jealousy.

Imagine the emotions in Hebe's heart! "I must go away from here," she told herself, "for what other remedy could there be for the sorrows I feel, and those I foresee?"

---

13. In the seventeenth century, duels were still the definitive way to resolve conflicts of love, despite several royal edicts forbidding them officially.

Meanwhile, the king and queen resolved to ask Atimir to set sail for his kingdom, to avoid the new turmoils his love might occasion; they would make the same request of the prince of Tranquility Isle, eager to show no preference. But—o untimely prudence!—as they were deliberating on the two princes' departures, the princes themselves were preparing for combat.

Coming home from the joust, Hebe asked where the prince of Tranquility Isle might be. She was told he'd been seen in the palace garden; he seemed very sad, and wanted to be alone. The beautiful Hebe thought it her duty to console him for the small disgrace he had suffered, and so, not troubling to stop by her rooms, she hurried out to the gardens, followed only by a few of her attendants. As she looked for the prince, she entered a shady pathway and happened upon Atimir. Transported by his passion and listening to its inspirations alone, he dropped to his knees a few steps away from the princess, then drew the sword he had received that day from her hand and said to her, "Hear me, beautiful Hebe, or else let me die at your feet."

Hebe's horrified ladies-in-waiting rushed forward to wrest away the sword he was even now desperately pressing to his breast. Poor Hebe wanted to flee, but are there not always a thousand reasons to stay at the side of the one we love? The desire to prevent the scandal this incident would cause, the need to urge Atimir to put behind him, if he could, a passion that was hurtful for them both, the pity roused by the touching spectacle before her—in short, everything held the princess exactly where she was.

She went to the prince. His fury calmed by Hebe's presence, he dropped his sword at her feet. Never had such anguish, so much love and pain been heard in a conversation of just a quarter of an hour. There are no words tender enough to express what those unhappy lovers were feeling. Hebe feared being seen in Atimir's company, particularly with the prince of Tranquility Isle so near, and thus, at the price of a great struggle, forced herself to leave Atimir there, ordering him not to approach her again for as long as he lived. What a command for Atimir to hear! Were it not for his imminent duel with the prince of Tranquility Isle, he would have turned his sword on himself a hundred times; but he was determined not to die without avenging himself on his rival.

Meanwhile, beautiful Hebe retired to her rooms, fleeing Atimir's presence. "Pitiless fairy," she cried, "you foretold only death for me if I saw that poor prince again; but the pains I now feel are far crueler than any mere loss of life." She sent one of her ladies-in-waiting to look for the prince of Tranquility Isle all through the gardens and the palace, but there was no sign of him anywhere. Poor Hebe was beside herself with alarm; they looked for him all night long, but to no avail, for he had hidden away in a rustic little house deep in the woods, to ensure that no one could stop him from taking part in the duel. Sunrise found him at the appointed place; Atimir arrived a few moments later.

The two rivals drew their swords, hungry to avenge themselves and claim victory. The prince of Tranquility Isle had never in his life used such a weapon, for war was unknown in his land. Nonetheless, Atimir found him a redoubtable foe; he had little experience, but a great deal of courage and a great deal of love. He fought like a man with no care for his life, and Atimir fully lived up to his reputation as a superb swordsman. The princes were animated by too many diverse passions for their contest to end in anything other than tragedy. The duel dragged on and on, with neither combatant holding the advantage, but finally they dealt each other two blows so fierce that they both collapsed to the ground, which was soon red with their blood. The prince of Tranquility Isle lay still and silent; mortally wounded, Atimir breathed Hebe's name as he died for her.

A few of the maidservants sent out to look for the prince of Tranquility Isle happened onto that scene, and stood stricken with horror at the terrible sight before them. Too fearful to go on waiting in her rooms, Princess Hebe had just come out to the gardens; she ran toward the sound of her servants' cries, vaguely making out the two princes' names, and so she soon found herself faced with that horrific sight. She was sure that the prince of Tranquility Isle was dead, like Atimir, and indeed at that moment nothing suggested otherwise. Gazing upon those two unhappy princes, Hebe cried out in sorrow, "Precious lives sacrificed for my sake, I will avenge you by taking my own!" And with that she threw herself on the fateful sword Atimir had received from her hands, piercing her breast before her stunned servants could come to her rescue.

She breathed her last breath, and the fairy Anguillette, moved by so many sorrows, which she had sought to ward off with all the obstacles her craft had taught her, appeared in that place where these beautiful lives had been taken. The fairy cursed the workings of fate, and could not hold back her tears. Then she set about saving the prince of Tranquility Isle, knowing he was not dead. She healed his wound and conveyed him back to his island quick as a flash. There, thanks to the miraculous power she had given that island, the prince found consolation for the loss he had suffered, and forgot the passion he had once felt for Hebe.

Having no such magic to help them, the king and queen lost themselves in their grief; time alone would console them. As for Ilérie, nothing can express her despair; for as long as she lived, she remained faithful to her pain and to the memory of the thankless Atimir.

Once she had transported the prince of Tranquility Isle back to his kingdom, Anguillette touched her staff to the heartbreaking remains of handsome Atimir and beautiful Hebe, transforming them into two trees[14] of the most perfect beauty. The fairy named those trees *charmes*,[15] preserving forever the memory of all the charms those ill-fated lovers once displayed.

---

14. Several myths evoke metamorphoses into trees, notably the story of Philemon and Baucis (Ovid 8.616–715). D'Aulnoy's "Le nain jaune" ("The Yellow Dwarf") also ends with the transformation of the two ill-fated lovers into trees (562).

15. A *charme* is a tree in the birch family known in English as a hornbeam. Alas, the etymology proposed here is fanciful; the French name derives from the Latin *carpinum*.

Works Cited in Headnotes and Footnotes

"Cornette, N." *Dictionnaire de l'Académie française,* 1694. *Dictionnaires d'autrefois,* University of Chicago, 2020, artfl-project.uchicago.edu/content/dictionnaires-dautrefois.

d'Aulnoy, Marie-Catherine. *Contes des fées suivis des contes nouveaux ou les fées à la mode.* Edited by Nadine Jasmin, Champion, 2004. Bibliothèque des génies et des fées 1.

———. "Le nain jaune." D'Aulnoy, *Contes des fées,* pp. 543–62.

———. "Princesse Carpillon." D'Aulnoy, *Contes des fées,* pp. 617–62.

Duby, George. *The Knight, the Lady, and the Priest: The Making of Modern Marriage in Medieval France.* Translated by Barbara Bray, U of Chicago P, 1984.

Duggan, Anne. "Women and Absolutism in French Opera and Fairy Tale." *The French Review,* vol. 78, no. 2, pp. 302–15.

La Force, Charlotte-Rose Caumont de. "Green and Blue." Seifert and Stanton, *Enchanted Eloquence,* pp. 213–30.

———. "Vert et Bleu." *Contes,* edited by Raymonde Robert, Champion, 2005, pp. 372–87. Bibliothèque des génies et des fées 2.

Molière et al. *Psiché: Tragédie-Ballet.* Pierre Le Monnier, 1671.

"Moor, N. [1a]." *Merriam-Webster Unabridged,* 2021, unabridged.merriam-webster.com/unabridged/Moor.

"Mouche, N." *Dictionnaire de l'Académie française,* 1694. *Dictionnaires d'autrefois,* University of Chicago, 2020, artfl-project.uchicago.edu/content/dictionnaires-dautrefois.

Murat, Henriette-Julie de Castelnau, comtesse de. "Anguillette." Murat, *Contes,* pp. 85–117.

———. *Contes.* Edited by Geneviève Patard, Champion, 2006. Bibliothèque des génies et des fées 3.

———. "L'heureuse peine." Murat, *Contes,* pp. 179–96.

Perrault, Charles. *Contes.* Edited by Jean-Pierre Collinet and Natalie Froloff, Gallimard, 1999.

———. "Les fées." Perrault, *Contes,* pp. 251–54.

———. "Peau d'âne." Perrault, *Contes,* pp. 133–57.

———. "Le petit chaperon rouge." Perrault, *Contes,* pp. 207–12.

———. "Riquet à la houppe." Perrault, *Contes,* pp. 275–83.

"Rayon, N." *Dictionnaire encyclopédique Quillet*, 1977. *Dictionnaires d'autrefois*, University of Chicago, 2020, artfl-project.uchicago.edu/content/dictionnaires-dautrefois.

Robert, Raymonde, editor. *Contes.* Champion, 2005. Bibliothèque des génies et des fées 2.

Seifert, Lewis C. *Fairy Tales, Sexuality, and Gender in France, 1690–1715: Nostalgic Utopias.* Cambridge UP, 1996. Cambridge Studies in French 55.

Seifert, Lewis C., and Domna C. Stanton, editors and translators. *Enchanted Eloquence: Fairy Tales by Seventeenth-Century French Women Writers.* Center for Reformation and Renaissance Studies / Iter, 2010. The Other Voice in Early Modern Europe: The Toronto Series 9.

———. Introduction. Seifert and Stanton, *Enchanted Eloquence*, pp. 1–45.